To anyone that has ever felt overcome by pain and afraid to live their authentic life. This story is for you. I see you. You can be exactly who you are and live however makes you happy as long as you are not hurting anyone. So much love and thank you so much for picking up this book xoxo

<u>More To Life</u>

Chapter 1: Bryce

It was setting up to be a sunny July day as my alarm went off for the start of another week. The evergreens were looking powerful and full of amazing color as the Pacific coast sun began shining through them, illuminating the area like a sea of ginormous Christmas trees. I ripped off my blanket and then hopped out of bed. I quickly put on my light blue collared shirt with a pair of gray dress pants, I rushed out the front door and into my car and headed up the freeway to the bustle of downtown for another busy day. Pulling out a banana and some apple juice for the ride which I had grabbed on my way out, a light breakfast is the best way to go. I never feel too hungry in the morning anyway, and by the time my lunch break comes, I usually get a delicious meal from one of the nearby Japanese cuisine restaurants. Having a more simple breakfast also allows me to set my alarm a bit later, for 5:45 instead of a painful 5:30. It may be only fifteen minutes, but being so close to 6 AM seems to make the morning dread not feel as grueling.

I have now been in the workforce for a few years, and sometimes I cannot believe how fast that time has gone by. So many of life's events can flash by you in an instant which is why at my age I am starting to fully embrace every moment. Understanding the value of really treasuring everything I get to do and appreciating all that I am blessed with is so important . I never know when someone I love may be gone for good which is why it is so crucial to fully embody the beauty of everything around you.

They say time starts to move quicker as you get older and, unfortunately, I think there is a lot of truth to that. It truly feels like yesterday I was just enjoying the festivities of my graduation from the University of Portland. Now, I have entered the mundane world of being an adult. I love my job, don't get me wrong, but life does start to get a bit less exciting after your college experience. Getting more mature does have its beauty though. You can see that life is more than just fun and games and being a working person in the world really does add value. I mean, I am still trying to live my life to the fullest, and it is always an exciting time to go out exploring places on the weekend, but I guess now the next big and awesome life event I have to be excited about is, hopefully, marriage. Until then though, I try not to get jaded by how tedious some of the days can be.

Being single at this age is sometimes confusing too. Part of me had imagined that in college the person of my dreams would come into life and that would be it. I would propose we buy a house a little outside Downtown Seattle and start building a family, but sometimes life does not follow the picture perfect path. I try to remind myself that we all have our unique destiny and it is important to know I am not behind and there is no official timeline in when things have to be accomplished. I even recently read a statistic that a third of American adults are single. That is a good chunk of people. Society likes to imprint on us that it is normal to find your soulmate in your early college years, get married, buy a house and then have kids. But for a minute can we just stop and remember that life is not just all about that? I mean love is beautiful, I completely believe that but there is so much more to life than just romance.

As I get older, I think the world portrays that image way too often because, if you think about it, there are so many people who get married in their 20s just because of the pressure. It then ends in a divorce 10 maybe 20 years later. In some ways, I am beginning to think there is a real liberation to not settling down so quickly. That does not mean part of me did not hope to find my true love in my early 20s, but fate had different ways. To start, for a couple of years there was a period when I thought I might be gay. I mean doesn't everyone try to find themselves more at college? Growing up, too, in the Pacific Northwest, where it is such an inclusive and accepting environment made me feel curious to explore. I even had a couple of good buddies from high school who were part of the LGBTQ community. Having people so open to being themselves around you leaves a beautiful impact on your heart. Even if you know people who may not be gay, and just are living out their full potential and being the exact authentic human they are. It is so inspiring to have people in your life that are so free in embracing their full purpose.

Well, soon after trying a couple of dates with a guy, I found out I definitely only like women, but it was a powerful experience to know if that was really who I was, then it would be completely okay. This, however, delayed my prospect in finding someone for a bit. Also, I have always been such a driven person. I really wanted to embrace the whole educational part of university as much as I can. I still had my fair share of fun experiences. From a weekend trip down to San Francisco to a week long ski trip to Colorado, I was lucky to have had the chance to live a little but I was someone who knew how precious life can be and how building a good future for yourself is so important. I think going through such a hard trauma when I was little really helped to put that into perspective.

My dad died from prostate cancer when I was only seven years old. It broke a part of me, but thankfully, I always wanted to use the pain and turn it into something good. I became determined to be the best version of myself, to never let my dad down. As I got older though, I started to realize my dad would always live on in my heart, and it should not be about worrying not to let him down. I definitely am a spiritual person and believe there is more to life than just this physical realm, so I have to live in a way that will make me happy and that is something I will be proud of. In high school, I was on the honor roll every year and wanted to keep that same ambition throughout college. I truly wanted to work hard to lead a full life, and it is safe to say dating was not my main priority. That ended up being okay, though I mean I truly believe all that hard work paid off. Plus, I live in a gorgeous state, work for a good company and life has been amazing so far. I get to go on at least one big vacation every year with the time off package.

I am not the kind of guy to wallow in self-sabotage. There is just so much good to focus on other than not having another person to love. Romance is a great part of life, but so is having friends. So is traveling on great vacations. So is going on adventure-filled hikes. And I will do my best to enjoy all the awesome things I am currently blessed with.

As I drove to work the greenery along the road was so bright everywhere I turned and the mountains nearby were covered in snow which made them look so mighty. The sun was making its way to the peak brightness and it began to cast its light on the puget sound and the nearby skyscrapers. It all surrounded the metropolitan area with a sense of beauty that a lot of cities do not have. It was like a little bit of heaven was here on earth adding some calm energy to what often can be a hectic week.

I pulled up to my job and made my way to the office. As I walked through the fresh air for a moment, I was able to catch a sense of true freedom, before heading into the confined space of corporate America. Once I made it to the floor which is like my second home, I ended up greeting a few of my co-workers including Crystal. Sometimes we hang out together enjoying some of the Seattle nightlife or even exploring the nearby nature, but I could never see myself dating her. We also hooked up a few times and let me tell you we both really enjoyed that. There should be no shame in having a bit of fun with your friend as long as you are both okay with it.

I really love spending time with her but she is not fully the type of lady I would be compatible with. In the long run, I got the feeling that it would end up not working out, so I had to tell her it is better just to stay friends. I mean I would not mind someone who likes to party a little extra, but Crystal is a bit of an extreme of a party animal. You can say I am more of a romantic sap. I like a lot of mushy sweet stuff and prefer someone who is a bit more boring. See that is why dating is so subjective like I know for sure Crystal will find a guy who loves her for who she is. However, Even though she is not my ideal match, she is such a joy to be around. Some of my best memories of being an adult have been captured with the two of us. Whether it be our weekend trip to Alaska we did back in April or just memories of us jamming to Green Day together driving along the freeway in her convertible. We have had a lot of exciting moments together that I am forever grateful to be able to store in my heart.

Crystal is a transplant to Seattle from a town in New Jersey right near the beach called Point Pleasant. She really seems happy a lot more often than most people. It is great to have a best friend who carries such a positive ray of sunshine. This may partly have to do with the fact that she is so much more happy to be on the west coast. I cannot even count the amount of times she has talked about her dread of the east coast. She is especially mean to her home state Calling it an overdeveloped, business infested wasteland, which cracked me up a ton. I guess sometimes a change of scenery to somewhere better can make a big difference.

I have actually visited New Jersey once. The summer after graduation from college, we took a trip to New York City and, for some reason, my one good buddy, Chris, was dying to see Atlantic City. Honestly, I think him being such a fan of the Jersey Shore show was the only reason why he wanted to go see it. He wanted to immerse himself in the party scene of that area which the coast of Jersey is famous for. He has always been more of a party animal than me, so I could also see why the Jersey shore was pulling him in for a visit. I have noticed people will sometimes be compelled to go somewhere after watching a specific area on screen. Like for me, last January I watched a movie called Call Me By Your Name and then that summer I booked a trip to Italy and took my mom along. The movie was so beautiful and was really a poignant gay love story that made me tear up and feel so many emotions. The setting, though, added a beauty that I had never experienced before. The setting which was filmed on location was beyond picturesque. Seeing it then made me want to have an Italian countryside getaway and boy did we have an epic one.

The beaches on the Amalfi Coast and the rock work all along the water was such a stunning sight to take in. It kind of reminded me of the coast up here in a way but with its own unique flare to it. A lot of European countries have cliffs by the water similar to the west coast, so that made it kind of more special in a way since I am a big fan of that sort of scenery. It was definitely a different kind of trip then I usually take but I feel it was good to change it up from my usual sort of vacations I do. Plus, that year I was not in the mood for an adventure-filled getaway like Orlando which we did on a trip prior. I usually prefer more action-packed trips but that year I really was craving a lazy one. I definitely was not feeling up to walking miles through the Magic Kingdom in the blazing hot sun. Do not get me wrong, the theme parks in central Florida are so amazing but work was crazy busy and I needed a more peaceful respite.

Who knows, maybe Chris just thought Atlantic City looked fun anyway, without any influence from that famed reality show. Even though we only spent two nights there, it was cooler than I was expecting. It was very business filled though, so there is definitely some truth to her jokes, but the beach there was actually really nice. We do not swim on the beaches up here much, so I guess that is a benefit to the East Coast. The boardwalk coming alive at night with all the amazing colors was incredible too. It felt like a rainbow array of flashy lights almost resembling a less elaborate version of the Vegas strip. I have been to a couple of boardwalks in Southern California, and they do not compare. It was an actual walkway made out of wood too. I will never now understand why people call a concrete path they have down in Venice Beach a boardwalk when it really is not one at all.

I guess that is one thing they do better out there. It was really something else seeing all the many stores, arcades and other attractions lined up along the boards of Atlantic City. I mean, if I am being honest, though sometimes it actually is quite inspiring in a way, because the way she talks so negatively about it makes me think maybe the West coast is the best one. I heard other out-of-town folk transplants trash the East Coast too, calling it just way too busy and fast-paced. I don't know if one is better than the other, but there are definite differences. I feel any state you live in will have good things as well as negative aspects too.

"Good morning Crystal " he says "Hey Bryce, you enjoy the weekend? "You know it, wish it could have lasted until this Friday though, what about you?" absolutely, living my best life here and enjoyed the beautiful weather we had. Have a nice Monday my friend ." I smile briefly before continuing my walk down the hallway to my desk which overlooks several other concrete buildings. Quick run-ins with her are always a great way to start the week. Having such a lovely friend who also works in this office makes coming here even more worth it.

I am also fortunate to work at such a good company. Seaside Programming is not a toxic work environment and all of my colleagues are pretty chill. Everyone seems to really just focus on the work and not let any additional drama seep into our busy days that are filled with making the softwares run smoothly. I appreciate people who do not add extra nonsense to life. We all deal with our own baggage, there should be no need for adults to overcomplicate things even more. I mean life could be a lot worse. Even though it would be nice to just travel all the time, I know there are much more terrible places I could spend five days in. If you think about it, my job is also a dream for someone else. There is somebody now out there who probably wishes they could have a computer job and is stuck doing some other one out of necessity. And at least I get to do something I enjoy to as much of an extent you can enjoy work. As I sit down and get set up for the day, I take a deep breath and log on to my computer ready to dive in and give it my all and make it through the Monday.

<u>Chapter 2: Carly</u>

I pull up to work a little hung over from the excitement I shared with my best friends. The leftover feeling from the eventful weekend comes upon me in a way that lets me know I had a good amount of alcohol. It was such a fun time with the girls, but these hangovers can really suck. I along with Britney and Sara drove down to Portland for some bar hopping and to enjoy some of the local rock scene. It can be fun to see a different city even if it is one just shortly across the state border. Portland and Seattle are not that different but changing up the scenery can be really fun. We have probably been to every concert bar and club in the city of Seattle now so keeping things fresh with seeing a different area adds a bit of excitement. The Rose City also is a bit less busy, which adds a more relaxing vibe. It really is like a smaller version of Seattle. With mountains, waterways and big evergreen trees everywhere you turn. It is a great place to just kick back and chill sometimes.

If I am being honest, getting drunk is fun once in a while, but live music is the best part of it all. Experiencing new artists at the smaller venues around the cities is always electrifying. Supporting independent acts is nice which is why sometimes I like to pick up a tshirt or physical album from their merch tables. I really have a lot of admiration for artists who are up and coming or just do it for a living without a major record deal. A lot of times smaller artists have amazing songs too. The excitement a good melody can bring is really so priceless. Spending a little bit of my cash to show some appreciation is the least I can do. One of the coolest parts about being a living person is getting to be able to experience the beauty that a good tune can bring. It is like when you find a good song, you are experiencing a bit of cosmic magic. In an instant it can change you into a happier mood or put you in a more reflective emotional state. Music just stirs the soul so much, drinking on the other hand, can leave you feeling like crap.

The Shooting Stars also ended up being an amazing band. They brought us to a magical place that made the room feel like we were transported to actually floating in space among the planets and galaxies. The mellow sounds of their voices and instrumental arrangements all felt so magical. The vibes all felt good and everyone there was really enjoying every second of feeling the sound waves from live music. A bunch of people were dancing the night away and singing their hearts out. It felt like at that moment everyone was free to just have the best time ever and be completely and unashamedly exactly who they were.

Even though I enjoy some rock, I am more of a Pop girl. Something about the bubbly and simple hook of a catchy song just takes you to a place of utter euphoria. During my teen years, Kesha and Carly Rae Jensen were two of my favorite stars. I cannot not even tell you how many times I have played Kesha's album Animal or Carly's one Kiss on my Ipod nano. Those two projects really showed how much magic can come from that sort of music. The escapist lyrics and cheerful melodies would latch onto me like nothing ever had before. I have always been a big music lover but those projects showed a new side of me and how much I really appreciated songs that can in an instant make you feel so happy. I have not done many drugs and quite frankly I do not need too because music gives me such a good high.

Despite not being the biggest rocker chick, they really ended up being so fun, especially for a local band. I even ended up buying one of their t-shirts and adding their album to my Apple Music library. It was such a rocking night with maybe just a tad too many Blue Hawaiians.

Despite feeling a little nauseated, I grabbed my purse and walked out of the car. At 25, I am full of energy, but I have always been a super bubbly person. It is just who I am. No shade to anyone who may be a little more serious but it is just not the type of personality I have been given. I do not let a little feeling of sickness bother me all that much. As the new week dawns my determination to take on the world of work after a fun time is strong. I have always been a free-spirited soul as well, loving life and not really into any cynical stuff. Working hard and playing hard has been my mantra since I graduated college. You cannot just have fun all the time and to be honest, would the fun feel as good if that was all you did? There is something special about working a long week then getting to live it up on the weekend. There is a sweet sense of fulfillment that adds a bit of light to what sometimes can be a stressful five days of using my skills to help the world.

Growing up in Santa Monica definitely played a part in the type of woman I am today. I love being a California girl and truly adore my hometown. Being around the glitz and glamor of Los Angeles was always amazing to me. It was not even about the celebrities, just being so close to the best film industry in the world, was so inspiring. It gave me a feeling like I can do anything I want and become whoever I was in my most true form. It is wild to think that some of the best movies were being created minutes away from my house. I also loved the nature that was nearby. From the beaches to the beautiful mountains the Los Angeles area as well as Death Valley National Park a couple of hours drive away. There was always something to do. From rocky areas to towering Redwood trees and the pacific coast highway, the whole state really is a spectacular setting. Despite what the media says a lot lately trash talking about my home state, there is no place like it. Moving up here was hard but part of me felt like there could be some good that would come out of it. It seemed like a fresh start after so many years in the same place is what fate had in store for me. My mom raised me to be someone who is not afraid to take chances and be a strong and fearless woman. Something in my gut was saying it is what I should do. We actually vacationed in Washington once when I was a kid and I remember it being beautiful. We visited Olympic and North Cascades National Parks as well as the Seattle aquarium. I just remember all the evergreen trees looking beautiful and thought it was amazing how the state was just covered in them as well as so many towering mountains. We drove up there and that added a special level of excitement that thirteen year old me was so amazed by. Driving on the pacific coast highway full of the epic nature that fills the area had that little girl I was, feeling so giddy. After doing so many trips camping at Yosemite National park, it was always nice sometimes to get out of that state and see other ones. I never could've imagined though that I would become a permanent resident outside of The Golden State.

The pay they were offering me was perfect. That definitely was a big driving factor in going forward with the move. None of the technology jobs in the Los Angeles area offered that good of a salary with such stellar vacation time. There was not too much of a selection to begin with and now that makes sense to me. I have recently learned from my friend Sara, that 80 percent of the jobs in my current city are those related to technology. Being a lifelong Seattle area resident, Sara always has a lot of fun facts about this city. I guess that's one perk to never moving, you become a total expert on the area.

I also thought maybe a change could be good for me. They say if you want to fully experience life, it can really help to move out of your hometown. It is not like I was moving to Kansas. The West Coast and Midwest are just so different. I do not know if I can be a Midwest girl ever. The miles of open corn fields, country music playing a lot and no coastline are just not for me. I do not know if I would fit in there that well. I guess some people are placed where they really are meant to live. Like you hear people in the south rave about where they are from and never want to move. It is important to live in someplace you love. Why be stuck in an area you are not happy with? The beautiful thing about our country too is there are so many living environments. You can really have whatever type of lifestyle you feel is best for you. From coastal areas to highly developed suburbs to a small mountain town, each state really has its own unique style where you can choose to live your best life. For me, I need the freeing, epic nature of this coast and the good-laid back vibes. Something about the towering mountains and mighty Pacific Ocean adds something epic to life. I am just a true west coast soul forever.

In the end, I am really happy I made the move. It may have been one of the best decisions I have made so far. Being in a new state has given me a confidence I never knew I had. In some ways, it almost made me feel like Superwoman ready to conquer whatever comes into my way. It was a little nerve wracking at first. When you live somewhere your whole life you do gain a sense of comfort. Then you leave all you have ever known for someplace completely new. Even just moving two states away on the same coast in America was a bit jarring.

There was a lot of unexpected goodness coming up here. I never thought I would say this, but I may have come to love Washington as much as California. The beauty here is breathtaking and the relaxed vibes still remain. It also appears a bit friendlier here, which was refreshing. I guess all the sunshine in Los Angeles does not add too much joy to life down there. Even though there is a six-month drizzle, a more cozy feeling is evident that is really sweet. I can see now why this area is so romanticized by many people. I feel ready to build a life up here and see what great things are going to come. California may be home, but here is where my future is going to be and what a nice place to have one in. Change can be terrifying, but everything happens for a reason. We are all placed exactly where we need to be at this moment.

As I make my way to the office, I then am reminded that in a few more days it will be time for another adventure. This weekend my friends and I are taking a trip down to Canon Beach in Oregon and my excitement is so great. I cannot believe it is just Monday though. I enjoy my job to an extent but cannot wait to be immersed in the amazing Oregon coast soon. Work can only be so good, but weekend adventures are what makes life worth all of this. As I arrive at my desk and log on to the computer, I see there is a lot of work to get done. Right now, the team is creating new software for Amazon. It is basically an updated version of a program to enhance the shoppers experience. It is going to recommend better products for their shoppers. You know when you log onto Amazon and see the recommended section for you? Yeah. We are basically making that better for them, which may not sound too hard, but it is really a lot of work. There are so many pages that need to be tuned and adjusted for it to be up to their standards. Something about computer programming really interests me though. I know it is a job and I kind of have no choice but to do it if I want to live. However, I feel there is really a fulfilling aspect to helping create or, in this case, improve software for companies. I feel, despite all the negative things people have to say about new technologies that have been coming out, there is a lot of good about them too. It can make the world better in ways and help make things easier too.

As the day finishes, I end up feeling exhausted and ready to go home. I packed up my things and put them in my tote bag. After I got home and had some leftover pad thai for dinner, I ended up opening my phone and doing what I do for about twenty minutes every night, some swiping on the Bumble app. I am not desperate for love, and I know that is not the end all and be all to life, but it is still okay to look. Being so busy with work and then going on outings with my friends pretty much every weekend does not leave much time for finding a man in real life. That is why dating apps come in handy. It shows you so many single people in the area, and you know they all want some sort of connection. A lot of times, though-that connection is just a one-night quickie or a long-term friend with benefits, but I still like to have hope. Sara found her man on Hinge, so I know it is possible. There are good guys out there looking for love, so you just have to be patient and see if the right one ever ends up falling into my life.

As I am about to finish swiping, I stumble upon a deliciously handsome man. Wow, he is hot. I pass so many good-looking guys though, so that is nothing too unique. I then continue to browse on his profile and feel drawn to it. He seems to not have the super assertive vibe to him that I have seen countless guys carry. Everyone has their own type and strong masculinity is just one thing I have not been drawn to, and quite frankly, that kind of stinks. A lot of guys carry that strong attitude. I also do not know how much of it is society's conditioning or just how men are and that is something I think about from time to time. Something about his energy, though, seems really sweet. Still, his piercing, blue eyes and wavy brown hair are two traits I find irresistible. At 5 feet 6 inches, he is a little on the shorter side, but who cares? Short kings can rule too. I feel like height in a guy is overrated too. Wanting a guy to be over six feet may just stem from women having the need to feel protected by their man. I do not need a boyfriend as a bodyguard. That is not my main desire in having a partner. I am looking for someone in whom we can embrace one another on a deep level. Oh! And he has a picture of him on Canon Beach. I need my man to be a nature lover. Because as much as I do not mind hitting up the bars and clubs, sometimes there's nothing like being out in the West Coast wilderness. As Carly scrolls down a little more she stops in shock for a second. In his employment info it reads "Computer Programmer at Seaside Programming." Feeling stunned for a second that we work at the same company, I do not know if I have ever seen him before. Could he be a remote worker? I know they have a few people now that work from home. Who knows? I smile and decide to definitely swipe right at this hottie. Then one second later, the screen lights up with a bold "It's a match" wording. I then quickly type

"Hey there, handsome ;)."

Without giving it any thought I clicked send.

Chapter 3: Bryce

The sun is still shining bright even at 6:30 on this warm summer evening, as I began my commute. I can be grateful today the traffic was not too bad which made the ride home feel like a breeze. I ended up getting some Burger King for dinner while enjoying a peaceful ride. I know the medium Whopper meal is not the healthiest thing but dang is it so delicious. Life is too short to not indulge in junk food from time to time. A moment later I noticed Mount Rainier is showing its beauty off for us tonight. I took in the full view of it as I passed over a bridge. That never gets old. The mountain is covered in snow pretty much always while towering around the surrounding area has just a magical quality. As it appears through my window I allow the majestic power it provides to fill me up.

Besides going to college in Oregon for a few years, Washington has always been home and the beauty of this state never gets mundane. I have heard of something that people living in tropical environments get called Island fatigue. It is like you get tired of seeing the same place for so long. I do not really understand that, because how can you get tired of living in such beautiful places? If Pacific Northwest fatigue is a thing, I sure have not caught it yet.

The scenery here even feels more epic than in the one state below and that is saying something. Oregon has such a special beauty too, but here, a little further north, it just seems more stunning. This may sound strange but, sometimes I think living here helps with my single hood. I mean seeing that there is beauty all around you in nature so much every day shows you that there is definitely more to life. I can definitely see why Crystal likes it more out here. I know New Jersey does have some nice parks, but it is nothing like the epic quality of it here on the West Coast.

After hopping in the shower and getting into my boxers, I end up doing what I do pretty much every night, play around on the Bumble app. As

I grow up I have started to realize much more that two things can be true at the same time. While being single is not the worst thing and I cannot control when the stars will line up right for my future wife and me to meet, it does not mean you cannot look. These dating apps can be a pain though. I mean I feel people just do not barely meet in person anymore. With inflation too and rent getting so expensive, it is like other singles do not prioritize dating anymore either. I get it though, I am busy too. Being an adult definitely differs from your teen years in the sense that there are so many more additional time-consuming responsibilities as well. It is just part of life though. Adulthood comes with many benefits too. Getting to have more power over your life and choose a career you definitely want is a good perk compared to being a kid. Despite my dad dying, which was pretty traumatic, my childhood was not really bad. My mom, Cathy, is such a wonderful person and made sure to give me and my brother Steven so much love. Mom lives in the Washington state countryside now though a bit of a drive away in a small town located not too far from Spokane. She has said while she loves her state, after 2020 a change was needed. The Seattle area just was not for her anymore, and she is definitely so happy out there. If I am being honest, Mom always seemed to be a country girl at heart. Having such a softness and sweet energy about her, I feel she may be always going to want to break free from the Seattle sprawl one day. I try to visit her at least once a month. There are so many amazing hiking trails we enjoy doing out there. It is always a fun time with mom, and I am grateful to the woman she is.

As I pulled up the Bumble app, I noticed I have gotten a new match with a message. I glanced over the profile of a woman named Carly. Reading her biography, it says, "forever a Cali girl at heart living in beautiful green Seattle, free-spirited, loves nature, music and comedy films, looking for my partner in crime to explore this beautiful world together and share an authentic connection. Don't be shy guys, if I message you let's see where it could go ;)) Well, she sounds fun. Then

I look over her pictures to get a better look, God, she's beautiful. With her platinum blonde hair and piercing brown eyes, something about her just stunned me. She had an all-American girl style that looked almost like one of those country singers. Kind of like a version of Carrie Underwood or Kelsea Ballerini but with a more fun energy to her. She definitely had an exciting but also laid back west coast energy too I could sense that just pulled me in. All of her profile pictures except one were in nature. Shots taken atop a mountain in Rocky Mountain National Park, snorkeling in the Great Barrier Reef in Australia. The one not in nature was at a concert for Katy Perry. Damn, this girl looks fun but also looks like such a sweet soul. Something about a nature-loving, fun, and gorgeous California girl is really getting my attention. I definitely can see why I swiped right on her.

I scroll down once again and become shocked by what I see next. " Computer Programmer at Seaside Programming." What? This beautiful woman works at the same company as me? Wait, oh my god, I have seen her before. One time we chatted in the break room a little about that new comedy movie I saw last summer. Wow. She must work on another floor. Our programming company has three floors in the office building in Downtown. They employ around 200 people. This is crazy though. My body fills with a bit of nerves, at first almost having a sense of intimidation by how cool she seems. It is very rare to see a dating profile that gives me such a level of intrigue. I sit for a moment on it and then, without any hesitation, I just go for it. I opened the message she sent

"Hey there, handsome ;)".

Seeing that makes me smile. Usually I'm sent the normal "Heys" or "Hi, how are you doing" from a lot of ladies. That made me happy to see her being a little flirty. Her even just adding that simple complement really seemed to brighten me up. I replied, almost instantly,

"Hey fun Cali girl, let us cut to the chase and waste no time. When can I take you on a date?"

It was like something bigger than me pulled me in to let go of fear and send the message. A sense of joy fills me as I remind myself I am enough, and I do not have to be scared. Maybe this random beautiful lady who possibly also works at my company, could be the start of an amazing chapter in my life. Or it could just be another conversation that dies quicker than an airplane making its full stop on the runway. The truth is, though, you never know til you try.

Chapter 4: Carly

As I pick up my phone from the nightstand I notice there is already a reply from Bryce. Quickly, I opened up the Bumble app and read the message. Damn, this guy really already seems so eager to meet in real life. In a way, this surprised me. A lot of times I will just be texting a man there for a few days, the conversation may be going okay, and then I get ghosted even before the first date. It is like I did not even exist to that person and in an instant I am just another forgotten bunch of pictures on a screen that they will never care to look at again. They disappear for whatever reason and never do I hear a word from them. It honestly is so disappointing. If I am being completely truthful, there is an element in dating apps that makes it even easier for people to treat you as disposable. It is like these days, people are so quick to move on without even trying to build something good. That must be why some say it is better to meet someone in person the old-fashioned way. I mean, I have had a few good dates but nothing has turned into anything serious yet. There was one guy named Alex who we had been fine, but from the beginning something about him seemed a little off. It did not help either that on the second date he already wanted sex, which I did not totally mind, but it showed he probably was just looking for more of a shorter fling. I feel like my generation is so open about embracing those shorter connections which, to be honest, are not always so bad. It is hard to find one human that you are authentically compatible with. Sometimes I realize though, it would be nice to have that one man to explore the world with. Like, call me naive but can't I just have one man to go on epic vacations with for the next, hopefully fifty years I am on this planet? It sounds so nice but seems like a real task to find, which is why lately I am learning to just enjoy all the fun times while they come and just let things happen if they are meant to be.

Bryce seemed serious already, that is a good sign. It is pretty rare for a guy to come off this strong. Even if it never ends up going anywhere, at least he is putting some effort in from the get- go to meet in person. A lot of people say it is better not to keep texting. If someone sparks your interest it is best to meet as soon as possible. I definitely agree that it is helpful to do. That is another reason I am so interested in him. Something about his direct attitude and showing pure interest off the bat is really sexy. Also, his profile having him listed as working at my company is intriguing. Who knows though, I mean he could have worked there for a month and never had the chance to update it. With so many dating profiles these days, it is better to know the facts rather than just jump to conclusions from their profile. One thing I was almost positive of was that he was a nature lover. I mean literally all of his pictures were taken at parks in Washington or Oregon, and that to me is an early green flag. I know that is not a common trait of good things to look for in a man but to me I have found some of the nicest guys were outdoorsy. There are plenty of nature lovers on the west coast, but he looked like a truly dedicated one. Fun and adventurous energy is a big thumbs up.

I was already starting to think of some ideas for our first date in my mind. Him being an outdoorsy guy, Discovery Park immediately came up. Ever since moving to Seattle, that place has become my favorite nature area whenever I need a respite. It is so beautiful with the dense evergreen forest and rugged coastline and only being a ten minute drive from my apartment, it is the perfect place to visit easily after a long day in the office. Sometimes a quick trip to just sit on the beach was the perfect recharge. With the gorgeous forest surrounding the water and going there as the sun began to set was always such a special experience that never became old.

I really think that could be a great first date idea. It being such a happy place too for me would alleviate any first date jitters. I just hope he will be OK with going next weekend. I still have that Cannon Beach trip coming up with Britney and Sara. That I cannot wait for, and I am so glad I have those two amazing friends despite whatever goes on with finding a partner. She then begins to type out her reply, "someone seems eager to meet. Well then, how would a trip to Discovery Park together sound like next weekend ;)" I smiled widely before sending the text. No matter what happens next, I know I am being exactly myself and in life that is the most important thing one can do. Putting her phone back on her night stand, she turns off her lights before slowly drifting off into dreamland.

The next morning, my alarm went off. As always, I try to hop right out of bed and not get too cozy. The world is waiting for me and every day is such a blessing. Thursday was here, which meant after today, only one more day in the office until Oregon. Canon Beach, here we come! Weekend trips are just the best. As my excitement is growing, I remember on my drive to work that there is a lot to get done today. The software that we are working on for Amazon had a big setback yesterday. As we were doing some of the updating, we had a password leak of about 5,000 users' information and Amazon does not like when stuff that involves their customers' personal data goes wrong. So today we are working on reversing the leaked information and have to check through a lot of information to see if any hackers got it then report back to their team. So that just added a load of extra work, but hey, it is what it is.

Nobody wanted this to happen. I enter the office and the team is already in a meeting room getting ready to go over a plan to get it all fixed. I can already sense the tense energy filling up the conference room. Being in the workforce now for a few years, it is days like this one which are about to come where she sees why being an adult can sometimes feel like hell.

After such a hectic day, I am so ready to head home. I pack up my things and sigh heavily as I walk down to my car. As I get older, there are some things about being a kid that just make life a lot easier. That innocence we all possess that a lot of adults lose really is just beautiful. Today, for some reason, that was plaguing my mind. Having the team just getting so frenetic over the leak really was just a lot of additional stress. It is partially due to Amazon because we are just hired as contractors to assist them. They already have so much to do for their company so they just use outside sources for additional help. Something like that going wrong just pisses them off. Then that energy makes all of our days feel like crap. As I walked into my apartment with the cloudy weather as the backdrop, the gloom was so warranted for the stress of today. There was not much emotional sunshine in my life today. Days like this make me see why some people can be so cynical about life. Why living is amazing but also at times it is unbearably painful. I thought to myself, why couldn't today just be Friday? I still have one more damn day of all that chaos. You can only hope tomorrow will be better, and hopefully the day won't feel too long because I am ready to be on the gorgeous coast curled up in a cozy cabin.

Chapter 5: Bryce

I begin my drive home from the office. Today the journey out from downtown did not start until 7pm. There were some extra software updates I had to do for Seattle's Children's Hospital and their patient charting program that the nurses and doctors use. I mean it was not an overly stressful day, but there was a lot to get done to finalize the program. We have to always make sure it is up to the standard they need. We are getting close to finishing it and that is always a great feeling. When we do something for one of our clients, there really is a great sense of joy and accomplishment that makes working feel worth it. Most of the staff we work with have a lot of gratitude and the team I am with at Seaside Programming are like a family. We are happy to have been championing each other well throughout getting all this work finished for the hospital.

As I drive along the freeway, the Seattle traffic is still pretty thick, but I peer out my windows and glance at the Cascade mountains and I am reminded there are much worse views one can have. The majestic Mount Rainier ends up making an appearance tonight. I am still in amazement to see the incredible presence it brings when it shows itself off to us locals. Despite being here pretty much my whole life, there is something about that mountain that still leaves me breathless. I mean to think about if I lived in New York City, the traffic views would be of mainly other buildings and, if I am lucky, a glimpse of the Hudson River. Here on my ride home I am surrounded by the dense evergreen woods and towering peaks. I guess that is one perk of west coast life. The dramatic mountains have once again left me awestruck, and I remember how grateful I am to be able to call Washington state home.

I pulled into my parking spot remembering I did not need dinner tonight. Crystal had ordered us some pizza back at the office. She was working later tonight too and decided to get us some Dominos to munch on. While we were eating, she said the only good thing about the East Coast is the pizza, especially in the New York City area. She believes though having a good pizza was not enough to make her stay out there. Plus, Seattle has some of the best Sushi. Dominos is pretty darn tasty despite it not being totally authentic so I am sure that is good enough for her. I do remember trying some of that New York pizza on vacation, and nothing here comes close to that deliciousness. I guess each region really does have a food they make the best.

After quickly showering, I hop in bed and grab my phone to play around on some apps for a bit. After looking at some travel vloggers' content on Instagram, I then checked Bumble. I noticed that the girl from the other day had messaged me back. It was really nice to see. I love seeing the interest she is already showing. I opened up our message thread and read her text

"Someone seems eager to meet, well then, how would a trip to Discovery Park together sound like next weekend ;)"

I smile with a sense of excitement. I have not been to Discovery Park in years. I think the last time I was there must have been when I was like 12 or 13. It is one of those things you take for granted. Being in this area for pretty much my whole life, I always want to get around to new places or to the bigger national parks where there are so many trails. I will not be able to hike them all in my lifetime. It is like I have forgotten to appreciate that right here in Seattle, we have a stretch of beautiful parkland. I think back to the last time I went there with my buddies, probably around first-year student year in high school. The bluffs there and the shoreline were so beautiful. Just being so young and free and truly appreciating the Pacific Northwest air for one of the first times is such a special memory. Something about her wanting that to be our first date just touched something in my heart and made me even more intrigued in this woman. Next Sunday could definitely work.

On Saturday, Crystal and I are going to do some hiking at North Cascades National Park, but there are no plans for that Sunday, so this is the perfect time to fill my calendar up for a date with a gorgeous person then. I started typing out a reply, "that sounds like it could be super fun, how does next Sunday at noon sound?". I did not even give a second thought before hitting send. I hope that will work for her because going back to that park will be so fun. Even if nothing comes out of this, and she thinks we do not have to take it even further, it is going to be special to visit that place again. Although, it would be nice if this could go further eventually. Let us just take it one moment at a time though. I then turn off my night lamp before starting to try and fall asleep.

<u>Chapter 6: Carly</u>

"Come on Carly, I want to get down to our Cabin already! It's travel time bestie!" Sara yells that joyfully as I walk down my stairs eyeing her 2022 blue Jeep. "Girl, I know! Can't wait! This is so exciting!" I hopped onto her ride, it's 6pm on Friday, and we are so eager to get going. Goodbye to the busy streets of the city, and soon we will be saying hello to the rural coastline. "I had to stop for some Coffee, cause you know what work will do to you, but after we get Britney, the weekend getaway begins!" " I look at my GPS and type in Britney's address to Evergreen Ocean cabins :"it is only a little over two hours from Britney's place, that really is not too bad." " I know it really is the perfect distance for a quick trip."

As we get closer to Britney's house Sara does what she usually will do and asks me how dating life is going. Sara is way more romantic than me and, quite frankly, just maybe, has had better luck so far. She met her now Boyfriend when she was a junior in college. They have been inseparable ever since. Johnny and she really do have a true connection, which is inspiring to see. It makes me realize too how love should look. I do not have time for any toxic relationships with a man who plays games. Life is just too beautiful to add someone in who will suck the life out of you.

They treasure and compliment each other's personality perfectly. They truly care about one another. Ultimately, they have that type of relationship that we all could only hope we will find. "So Carly, how has the dating game been going for you? Seeing any lucky guys now?"

I sighed gently before going "I mean Sara, you know how I am. I sometimes look, but it is not my biggest priority, nothing official yet. if I meet the right man and the stars line up for it to work, then so be it but for now I am just grateful for such an awesome life. You and Britney fill it with tons of fun and I am forever lucky for that." Sara gave a gentle smile. "Well, I really do hope they line up, and I have a strong feeling one day they will. I also know it will have to be a special man for that to happen because you are a truly amazing soul." I cannot help but to smile so widely. "I love you so much." "Love you too bestie" she replies.

As we pull up to Britney's house I see she is already standing outside with her bag. Britney is more Type A, she loves having things planned in a perfect schedule. That actually works out great for all of us. Having her being such a planner has been one of the best unexpected blessings. On our girls' trips she is the one to Google the restaurants and find other activities that we will do. Spontaneity is good in life but so is having some things planned out. She has really shown me that in a special way through our friendship.

Britney opens the back door and hops in," I see you guys made it on time, which is great, you know how I can get." I chuckled and replied "We know Britney, but we still love ya girl, how have you been lately?" "All good! Same old work

stinks, so I need this weekend." Sara and I look at each other and smile, then Sara replies "Well, that is what friends are for! We got you! It is going to be a great time to unwind!"

I then hit the big GO button on the maps app. Evergreen Ocean Oasis, here we come. As we near our cabin, the Oregon coastline began to make its dramatic appearance in our car windows. Giant boulders and forest surrounded the rugged pacific and we all stared in wonder. For me, I am more of a newbie to this area so I think I feel an extra sense of amazement. Compared to the palm trees and cliffs of Southern California, this region has such a distinct rustic quality that it really earns its spot as a setting in manu Hollywood romance movies. After the two-hour journey, we made it to our destination. We walked into our rental not being able to see much outside, it being so dark in the dense Oregon woods. I know from the website link Britney sent us, it has an ocean view but at this time it is hard to see much. We set our bags down, change into our pajamas, then hop into bed. We know it is time to get our rest for an exciting day of exploring the beautiful area tomorrow.

I get up a little before sunrise, and I am lucky enough to catch a beautiful coastal one. The bright yellow slowly begins to appear over the world's largest ocean. While that is happening an epic sense of power just fills me. The mighty Oregon wilderness is such a special place. As the sun makes its way up into the sky, the dense evergreen woods become visible. Their beauty never ceases to amaze me, especially being so absorbed in them while staying in a rustic cabin. Sara and Britney soon wake up after, and we get ready to head to breakfast. One thing that is so awesome about having Britney as a friend is she always plans the most amazing places and best restaurants on our trips. She found us a little spot this time for today's first meal called The Coastal Hideaway. She said their restaurant overlooks the ocean and has yummy food. So I am very excited to check this spot out. The excitement filled my spirit as we took the 20-minute trek over to the establishment.

The friendly staff greets us as we enter. There ends up being only other people in the tiny place. An older man is sitting at a table and smiles and waves towards us as we walk towards the table. I realize he is probably just lonely as sometimes elderly people are not blessed with as many people still here with them. Plus, if he does happen to live in such an isolated area, that would not make the situation better. The place has such a beautiful view. With cliffs around it and the outstanding lush greenery, I assume this is truly a hidden gem.

Well, the food I had ordered did not disappoint, and it had such a charming and quaint astechic. I enjoyed some scrambled eggs that were made with mushrooms and onions. I also got a side of turkey bacon with a fresh pressed apple juice that tasted better than any other juice I have ever had. It tasted as if they picked some apples right off a tree that morning at a farm down the road and put them right into the juicer. So fresh and delicious.

After breakfast, we did some hiking at a state park that is pretty close to the coast. The trail eventually leads to a beautiful view of the Grand Pacific. After we hiked for about a mile and a half, we hit a bluff in the woods that looks out over the ocean. As the Oregon breeze hits my face, a sense of peace covers my soul that consumes me every time I am out in nature. We just stood there together soaking in the gorgeous view of the mighty ocean. The waves crash onto the shore and I just think, man, the views of the coast do not ever get old. No one else is there besides the three of us and the secluded feeling makes the moment feel even more immersive. No distractions. Just the ocean, forest and two of my favorite people in the whole world.

We definitely are saving the best for last today because now we are heading over to enjoy Canon beach until sunset. We arrive there and pull the beach chairs out of Sara's Jeep. I stop for a minute to just take in the beauty and the epic nature surrounding us. The giant boulders in the water and forest everywhere are just stunning. A group of seagulls flies by looking like what freedom feels like. Sometimes I think it would be so nice to be a bird, to just fly and be in nature all day. It must be a special feeling. The charm of it all is so delightful. There is something special about Oregon that words will not ever fully be able to explain.

We are sitting down in our chairs just soaking in the beauty of this day. Soon, the sun starts to set, and we take in the beautiful image of the sky making its way back into darkness. It is a bright yellow mixed with orange, getting smaller, almost like the flame of a candle beginning to dissipate. As I soak all of it in, I just smile and say to my friends ``What a beautiful world we have been given, being out here with you guys, this is the best thing ever.''

The next morning, the girls and I load up the Jeep to start their trek back to Seattle. After packing up all our things, we had one last stop before heading home; another breakfast spot. This restaurant is in a town right near the Washington state border and is known to have the best seafood omelet and also some amazing fresh squeezed juices including a signature, ultra fresh cranberry, pear apple one..." I don't know about you two, but I am dying to try this place" Britney said as she hops into the back seat. "You literally always find the most amazing restaurants, I'm sure it is going to be amazing." I replied. "Are you guys ready to jet?" says Sara. Before we know it, we are driving away from our cabin down an evergreen filled country road. As we pull away, a little sense of sadness fills my heart as our cabin gets further and further away. I realize we are heading back up to urban Seattle and out from true nature. This has been such a fun trip and I wish I could just freeze this moment. There is nothing like being in the beauty of the Oregon wilderness. Why does time always have to move so quickly? It is always the best things too that seem to buzz by the quickest. As I realize the busy work week will be dawning upon me soon, I remind myself that you cannot freeze time, time will always move on, but experiences like this will live on in my heart for as long as it is beating. As long as I'm alive there will be more adventures, but something about this one leaving hit me hard. I wish we could just stay at Canon beach a little longer.

As we neared the Seattle sprawl, I realized a major civilization was nearby. "Britney, that seafood omelet was the bomb." "I know, right?! It was so good!" "Thank you for always finding us the best food. If it was not for you, Sara and I would probably be eating at Wendy's and Taco Bell for every meal." We soon pulled up near my complex and saw home sweet home was waiting for me.

"That was so fun Carly, I really had a blast! I hope you enjoy your week coming up! " Sara said "It was so much fun. I hope you guys enjoyed yourselves too. I replied. I smiled at them both before leaning over to give Sara a hug. I am a big hugger and she is too. It may be a little sappy but pretty much after every hangout I give her a huge one "Bye guys, get home safe! We will talk soon." I then hopped out of the car and waved as the Jeep pulled away. As I walked upstairs and into my apartment, I then slowly opened the door. Dread comes into me as I remember I am back to reality. My mind is already thinking about where our next weekend trip will be.

A few moments later, after I unpack, I pop down on the couch. I really want to watch the new episode of Stranger Things. I have a few episodes left of the third season. I get the hype now for this show. Even though I am a bit late to it all, better late than never cause it really is so fun. I end up turning on Netflix and enjoying the fun and eerie vibes of the show for a bit. After that, I pulled out my Iphone.I had barely looked at it at all over the past few days. When I am in nature, it is time to disconnect from the digital world. I soon realized there was a message from Bumble. I see Bryce did reply.... "That sounds like it could be super fun, how does next Sunday at noon sound?" Oh, that is so sweet. I think noon will work just fine. I began to type out my reply "that would be great :) so noon it is then, meet you at the lighthouse?" I then hit send and just closed out that app. I then move over to the photos section already looking at the pictures from Oregon. Just remembering how magical that weekend was. Looking back through pictures of the lush moss drenched forest and one of me and my best friends in the whole wide world taking a group selfie on the beach. I tell myself that no matter what happens with this guy, I am so grateful and going out and enjoying life with Britney and Sara is already a lot more than most people have. Friends like this are a rare thing too, just like finding your ideal partner.

Chapter 7: Bryce

I sat on my balcony with the cool evening breeze coming up against me and the Northwest sun beginning to set. The sky still had a subtle brightness which made the greenery everywhere still visible casting the stunning, rustic forest vibes in whatever direction I looked. As I sat there enjoying the peaceful moment, I began to reminisce about the fun time I had recently. The weekend was so fun. I cannot stop thinking about it. Crystal and I took one of the most extreme trails I have been on in the North Cascades and what an epic adventure that was. Trying out new trails in the national park is always so exhilarating. I keep thinking of that view we made it to. With the wide open area that shows the snow-capped mountains and just the fresh air that makes you feel alive. It really was an incredible experience. I chuckle too, remembering when we made it there what Crystal had said, "You will never see a sight like this in Jersey. There are so many warehouses and pizza joints they put up anyway that would block any nature." She and those New Jersey-hating jokes always get me. It was such a fun weekend and something about Crystal's energy always makes things brighter. I realize too how cool and rare it is to have a woman who is just my friend. As a guy, this is not as common of a thing, but I am so grateful for our pure connection.

As I walk inside and look at my phone, I look at some Instagram Reels of a travel vlogger I love. SamsWorldTravels always has some great content. He recently took a trip to the Maldives and the short showcasing of the island is just stunning. The baby blue clear waters and palm trees just look so gorgeous. If Heaven looks like anywhere on earth, I would not be surprised if it resembles this place. I really think my next big trip is going to be out there. Even though it generally is a more expensive place to visit, I am going to make it work. Life is too short to not act on something that is calling your heart. Besides, with most places there is a way to find reasonable accommodations.

I then popped over to another reel on his instagram page, and it shows one highlighting a Las Vegas hotel called Resorts World. The reel begins to play and gives us an amazing view of a few of the hotel's multiple lavish pools, the many delicious restaurants and the beautiful concert hall where some of the biggest artists have played. Seeing this makes me want to head back to sin city. There really is so much to experience there and it is the ultimate tourist trap. Though in a good way, because what a fun trap it is.

Back in summer 2019, I finally made my first trip down there. I actually decided I had wanted to try a solo vacation and thought what better place to do my first one than Vegas? There are endless activities there and shows to see, and I had a feeling it would be a fun few days to have by myself. Well, all I can say is there is no place in the world like it. With the massive resorts everywhere you turn with such lavish designs, it really is a unique vacation spot. Then, the first night I was there, when all the lights came on outside the strip, I could not believe my eyes. It was like you were in a whole different colorful, exciting, glitzy world in the middle of such a dry desert. The shows and restaurants I got to see were all unforgettable. The buffet inside the Wynn hotel was some of the best food I had and Lady Gaga's live performance was simply out of this world. Seeing this post really brought back all the feels from a true live-it-up solo vacation I had.

I then move over to the Bumble app and see there is a notification. I look over it and see it has a red "1" mark, which could mean I either have a new message or a match. I open it up and see it is that beautiful woman who I have been texting with for a bit now. There is a new message from her. I opened and read what she wrote, "that would be just great :) so it is noon then. Meet you at the lighthouse?" I smiled brightly. The image of that building pops into my head. My mind began to flood with memories of it from that one time I had been over there. My buddies and I tried going in, but unfortunately it was locked. I remember thinking how cool it would have been to go inside there. To get a view of the Puget sound and how maybe we could see some pirates come in. Oh, I was such an adventurous young soul.

The lighthouse really is a perfect meeting spot. I think back again to the last time I went to Discovery Park, and how it looked so cool. It also represented the adventure-filled vibe of the Pacific Northwest. A land of natural wonders in every direction you turn. With cliffs, mountains that seem to reach endlessly up into the clouds and trees that seem to have gotten so big, it seems unnatural. The lighthouse is a sign that adventure abounds. I begin to type out my reply "That would be great, the lighthouse is a great spot to meet, so I will see you next Sunday :)" I then press send and a feeling of excitement fills my body. I do not know what will come out of this, but I have a sense this is going to be a fun date.

Chapter 8: Carly

"What should I wear Sara?!" I frantically asked her on a FaceTime call. "I mean it is a date out in nature, will I look bad with my hair in a bun with some jeans and a T-shirt, I cannot wear a dress when we will be out hiking and hanging out on a beach." Saturday was already here and the date with Bryce was drawing near. My excitement and nerves were mixed together at an all time high. No matter how many first dates I have done, there still always is a bit of anxiety. "Yes, a t- shirt and jeans is fine, I am sure he is not going to expect you to wear a dress and heels looking like a celebrity heading out to a five star restaurant while you will be in the middle of the woods." "I know it's just I have never done a first date at a park, so this is new." "Do not overthink it my friend, if he does not like how you are dressed then he obviously is not the one for you." Sara is absolutely right, I feel like people are always overthinking stuff about dates. I realize the best thing is to just be yourself. I mean in life, the only thing you can control is your own actions. The rest is up to something bigger. Most certainly fate does have a plan for all of us. I have to set all expectations down and just be my true self. It is love I am looking for and how can you attain that if I do not show someone all parts of yourself. I think such a special part of life is letting people that are meant to come to you, arrive with you being your authentic self. If you are being someone you are not just to get people to like you, in the end you can cause so much damage to only yourself. Wasting my life trying to please others is something I never did and I will not start doing it now.

The sun began to set after a lazy Saturday. I hear my doorbell ring and realize my DoorDash order is here. For dinner tonight, I will have some sushi rolls. I realize from living in Seattle now for three years that they really do have some of the best seafood. I mean the Los Angeles area does too, but we also have some great Mexican food too. If you are a huge sushi enthusiast like me, then Seattle is the place to be. I devour the delicious Tuna and Eel rolls before cleaning up my dining area. I could eat that every day. It was so delicious. I then went over to my couch and felt in the mood to watch a movie tonight. I open up Netflix and find a fun romantic comedy to watch. Something about this genre is just so fun. The escapism and humor in a lot of them are just irresistible. I hit play and soak in the fun of it, deep down putting myself into the character, hoping one day I can have my own sweet little real life rom com.

I woke up the next morning with a bunch of birds chirping in the giant evergreen tree near my window. I look at my Iphone and see it is already 10:15 AM. Damn, I do not usually sleep that late. Usually, even on the weekends, I usually wake up at 8 AM. I remember now too, I have to be at Discovery Park in less than two hours. For breakfast, I hop a sesame seed bagel into the toaster. I then do a little vacuuming around the place, and before I know it, 11:30 hits the clock, and it is time to head out over to the park. As I drive down the road and head towards the destination, a little bit of nerves fill my heart. Even at 25, and going on several dates, you would think I would not be nervous, but I do not know if that will ever go away. I mean to be honest, it is a stranger you are meeting online. Even though I do not expect him to hurt me, first date jitters are really normal, I do assume.

As I pulled into the more dense evergreen forest, I began to see a lighthouse appear in the distance. I have passed it many times during my visits here and it adds such a mystical vibe. Lighthouses are a sign of guidance too so maybe, for some reason, us meeting over here is a sign that I am on the right path. I pulled into the parking area and spotted a man standing right outside it. I think it could be him. Like why else would someone just be standing there so still? As I walked out of the car and moved closer to the lighthouse it was hard not to realize the handsome man is Bryce. "Well hello there Carly." I smile and reply "Nice to meet you Bryce."

Chapter 9: Together

Carly and Bryce begin to walk down towards the beach at Discovery Park. The physical attraction they have for each other is already so palpable. Bryce keeps looking down at the sand to not seem too much like a creep, but it is hard to keep his eyes from such a stunning woman. Her platinum blonde hair and beautiful face looked even more gorgeous than the pictures as the sunlight shines down upon her. She then glances over and gives him a light smile. He cannot help but to smile back. There seems to be already a pure sweetness going on, which they both find so adorable.

A moment later her soft voice breaks through the awkward silence, "So have you ever been here before Bryce?" "Only once, when I was around 12 years old, me and a couple of my buddies came here just to hang out. It was one of the first times that I really started to appreciate the nature of the Pacific Northwest." A flock of birds then fly out to the water as the two of them continue strolling along. Beauty is everywhere around them, and while they are both getting lost in their own little world, they also feel that they are about to get lost in some lovely nature that the earth has blessed us with.

"That is so cool, I mean we do live in such a gorgeous part of the country, it is great to appreciate it, have you always lived up here." "Yes, pretty much for all my life Washington has been home. I did go to college in Oregon for a few years, but that is it. What about you? I think If I recall correctly you are from California?" Carly smiles and replies "Yes, grew up and went to university in the Los Angeles area. "So how does So- Cal compare to the pacific northwest?" "Oh, it is like a completely different world but I actually adore it up here. Growing up down there, near the heart of such a big entertainment industry it is just different. You have so many people who are just trying to be famous.

Want to hear something crazy? One time when I was like 14 we were eating at a restaurant near Hollywood boulevard and someone came up to my mom thinking she was a famous talent agent, mind you she doesn't even work in the film industry! I guess they really were devoted to becoming an actor ""That is literally wild! People do say Los Angeles can be a weird place and now I think with that situation you have shown that is true " "Right? Like I will always love California, do not get me wrong, it is beautiful and the southern part of the state has such nice vibes with all the palm trees, but it just seems a little less strange in certain aspects here in the Seattle area, which is a good thing."

"I love California too, I mean what a cool place. They have the pacific coast highway, the redwoods, San Diego, and so many other cool places in one state, I definitely would love to visit there again one day." "There is so much epicness in one state! It is quite amazing. I usually go back home to visit around once a year, you know I got to see the family but it's fun because we usually get out to do at least one fun place while I am down there." "I'm so jealous, so I'm wondering how a fun California girl ends up here in the forest filled Evergreen State?"

"A few years ago, I moved up here for a job at a computer programming company." Bryce stops walking for a second, which leads Carly too as well. Then a spark of excitement goes off in his mind like a firework exploding on the Fourth of July. "Oh my god yes, that is right, you work at Seaside Programming, is that correct?" he asks. "Yes, I do, when we matched on Bumble I saw in your biography it said you work there too; is that accurate?" "Yes I do! Been there five years now, got the position shortly after graduating from college. Seemed like the perfect fit, to take that position before heading back home from Oregon. I knew I wanted to come live here again." Carly stops on the beach feeling a little shocked. "I just find that so fascinating, like how you can work with someone, and they can be right by you everyday, and you do not even know it." "I mean our company is pretty big, they do have three floors in the office building." "Yeah that is true, so how do you like working there?" "It is good. I mean my coworkers are all chill. Cannot complain "" "Yeah, I feel pretty similar, it is just work, but it could be a lot worse and at least the management is cool. They give us a lot of space. Cannot deal with any uptight bosses. I would not do well in that type of environment." "You and me both buddy." Carly says with a big smile.

Her mind is fascinated by the fact that they both are at the same company. It got her thinking how absorbed in the phone she can be and how this handsome and sweet guy has been feet away from her for probably a few years now. It is quite interesting, it seems people do not meet in person much anymore. I mean one does not expect to meet the love of your life at work, but it is good to keep your eyes open, not stuck down swiping on a digital software application. Someone really cool has been feet from me day in and day out for a few years now. At least now we are finally having the chance to meet and have been brought together for some reason.

Carly and Bryce make their way over to the bluffs with the afternoon sun blazing in the sky. The cliffs set along the sandy beach brings a sense of enchantment, and the beautiful rustic nature makes its grand gesture just minutes away from the urban sprawl. A large German Shepherd runs along with some owner creating a sense of true freedom. "Wow, I really forgot how beautiful this park is, it never ceases to amaze me, as well as how gorgeous nature is so close to the heart of downtown Seattle ", Bryce says. "I know, it is amazing right? I absolutely love this place, I usually stop by at least once a week just to relax." "Well, that is so cool. I should start doing that, sometimes a quick nature refresher makes the soul feel so much better." "I do agree with that, nature is the best therapy plus it is free, and i'm sure you know Seaside does not offer the best health insurance packages for us." Bryce chuckles, "they really don't, but what are you going to do? I guess no work place will ever be perfect!"

Bryce takes off his backpack he brought along and begins to unzip it, "Carly, is it okay if I take out a beach blanket,I brought it to relax if you are interested." "Sure, that sounds really nice." Bryce then begins to unfold it and lay it out on the white sand of the Washington state beach. "Brought some potato chips too and some soda if you'd like as well." He smiles and sits down next to his backpack on the blanket.

Carly cannot help to think about how sweet this is. She had never been on a date where the guy was this chivalrous. To be honest, she did not even know if big romantic gestures were something her soul would appreciate. Oh but now, though, she sees that she loves them. It got her thinking too how beautiful it is to be out in nature with a cute guy and be completely off technology. It really is a great feeling. Carly then takes a seat on the blanket as well and looks out over the water. "Want to go for a swim?" She playfully teases. "I once read here the water around our state does not usually peak 60 degrees and I ain't a penguin, so I will gladly pass." "You are not a penguin, but you sure are cute like one" she replies in a flirty voice. "Well thank you." "You are quite welcome Bryce."

The two of them chat and flirt on the blanket for hours, and the sun slowly begins its descent. The conversations ranged about everything from their favorite travel spots to the annoying reality of dating apps. "Yeah I really do love what you were saying about dating now Carly, a lot of people on the apps can be so picky and quick to move on, we are living in a world now where everyone seems to think they have endless everything." "Right, but the reality is we don't, and we are all finite, we don't have forever to love hard in these bodies so if someone comes along and appreciates you, and you do too then I believe it is important to give it a shot." " You are a special person Carly and I have never said this before on a first date, but I am surprised you have not been scooped up by a man yet." Bryce is amazed by the heartfelt wisdom that fills her soul. It is almost like she is a 70 year old trapped in a younger woman's body. Wise beyond her years for sure does already seem to be a good way to describe her.

Carly smiles and then lets out a sigh "but you see the thing is your worth, my worth or anyone's worth does not change just because someone did not choose you as their one and only yet, I mean life is just such this exciting, messy, crazy and beautiful thing, but sometimes it is like will one other person ever see my worth on a deep level" "I do Carly, no matter where this dating game goes, whether it all adds up and makes sense for us to be together or if it does not, know that you have one of the purest and beautiful souls, and I know it may sound crazy because we just met, but you can sense things sometimes, and I have never had a date go on for this long and with having such beautiful conversations like we have had, so thank you for today." "Well thank you too Bryce you are quite the special gentleman yourself."

They begin to make their way to their cars as the sky begins its transformation to darkness. They look into each other's eyes before Carly begins to say "Thank you for such a fun time, let's do this again." She winks at him and makes her way back over to hop in her car. As Carly begins to pull out and begin her drive home, Bryce keeps popping back in her mind. She cannot help but smile and realize that was the most fun she has had with a guy in a long time and also realizes amazing first dates like that do not always happen. The spark between them is strong, but then again, he is still basically a stranger from the digital world and feels like taking it slow is important.

Chapter 10: Bryce

"You finally went on a date again, I felt like that was never going to happen" Crystal says to me in the break room at work. "Yeah, it has been a while but it happened, and it went pretty well. In all honesty, it was the best first date I have ever had." "Tell me what did you guys do?" "Just hung out at Discovery Park, did some hiking and relaxed on the beach. It was a super peaceful time. "Ooooh that sounds so exciting and sexy." "Sexy?! You think? I feel like it was more exciting and rustic per say." "I mean it can be sexy too, you are such a hottie, so you bring that sexiness with you everywhere. And this lucky lady got some one on one time with your handsome face." I rolled my eyes. Crystal is so bold, she has such a north-east personality, and I love it. Her direct attitude reminds me of the stereotypical New York City person you always hear about. I know she means well though and her humor adds so much fun to my life. Being around her brings a sense of fun. It makes me feel as happy as being on a beautiful beach in Florida surrounded by crystal clear, blue water and gorgeous palm trees.

As I walked back over to my desk I remembered that Carly was right there in the same building. God, I really want to get to know her more. It has been a few days since that incredible first date and I cannot wait to spend some more time together and see where this all will lead to. I really feel like she is someone worth getting to know. You can just sense when somebody is actually looking to build a connection. Like there are a lot of people my age that still want something more casual. People can play games sometimes too and I do not have the energy for that. I really am feeling drawn to her. I then pop out my phone before I sit down and send a text to her; "Hey Carly, how have you been?" I then get back to work and my mind drifts into the busy world of computer programming. As I am focused on the screen at my desk throughout the day, Carly still keeps coming into my mind. It is like a little popcorn kernel that goes off every so often. I then realize I have never had a lady keep coming into my mind this much.

I get home and pop a frozen pizza into the oven for dinner. I looked at my phone and saw a text from Carly. "Been great, hope you had a fun time last weekend." I then typed out my reply, "Sure did, when can we do it again?"

I take my pizza out of the oven and cut it into slices. I then hopped over to my couch and started an episode of Stranger Things. Even though I have watched every episode, this show has good rewatch value. It really is such a cool series and I definitely understand why it became such a pop culture phenomenon. The 80s vibe is so dope too. I do not know why but the 80s just seemed like a cooler and more fun time compared to the 2020s. I mean yeah they had AIDS and a lot of hatred towards the LGBTQ + community as a result of that, but overall it seemed like a happier moment in history. I mean just look at the hit movies of the times. Then they had Ghostbusters blowing up. Now we have a film like Oppenheimer finding its way into current culture. So different.

As I finish the pizza, then the episode finishes. I checked my phone for the time and saw another text from Carly, "What about this weekend coming up? I'm free either day." I then texted out "Saturday would work great, any ideas of where you want to go next?" Before I hit send a little nerves start to fill my chest. Getting to know someone this cool can be scary. There is such a sweetness about her soul. I just hope I do not mess this up. I then gave a sigh of relief before pressing send.

Chapter 11: Crystal

I will never forget the day I officially met Bryce. We were in the break room and I had thought he was just so sexy from the first day I saw him walk past me. With his wavy brown hair and beautiful blue eyes to go with it, he was definitely one of the hottest guys there at our company. I had seen him before too interacting with others around the office and he seemed like a really friendly person. Often smiling, being polite to all of his colleagues and working hard. I even noticed him one time really helping out this other guy. He needed some help with the updated version of Xcode we had installed on our computer and Bryce was right there beside him helping out with some confusion he had with navigating it. Our boss only sent out one email with some of the new instructions so we did not have a formal training course. I can definitely see why some people may have been a bit overwhelmed. It still was such a sweet gesture he did. I would always think when I saw him that his energy felt like a different kind of man. It just seemed like he was ok with being the nice guy which can be rare for men. I then just decided to see what would happen if I tried to butter him up with a compliment, "Nice smile" I had said while he was sipping a glass of water and he immediately brightened up like it was the first time he ever got a compliment he then kept saying thanks and how sweet I am and I just found him so utterly cute. He really does have such an adorable smile. I feel like that represents all the joy that is in his soul.

We traded numbers and later that night I sent him a text. There was definitely some chemistry there and not too long later we started hanging out. Now, let me tell you the truth, my heart was so set on marrying that man and having a family with him, I wish it could still happen but apparently I am too much of a wild child for him. One sided love is probably one of the most frustrating things in life. It makes you second guess if you are enough but in the end, I am who I am and the rejection from Bryce actually allowed me to further accept all parts of my whole being. I now believe if something is not meant to be, there is no need to force it.

Maybe it is the Jersey in me, because from about 16 til I moved out here after college, I was a hard partier. From Atlantic City to Seaside Heights, from house parties to the many nightclubs on the Jersey Shore, I loved that scene. That wild night life-loving part of me has stayed in my soul all the way out here to Seattle. I learned that here the party scene is thriving. Although there is more of a grunge style vibe going and not as much of an EDM one as they have back out on the

East Coast, I have learned to enjoy the punk clubs. Bryce and I go to some together, and it is always a blast. I always try to loosen him up more. I can often tell he has a lot of deep things on his mind. Once the music gets going, like maybe four songs into the set, he gets swept away in the fun.

I definitely do not miss the north-east though, the hustle culture up there is real. Especially in the tri-state area (which does not include Pennsylvania, despite what a lot of people think. Just Jersey, New York and Connecticut.) I once had a good friend back there named Jamie. She grew up in Alabama, and then we met while I was at college back home, and she was so tired of the south. She would go on about how New Jersey had so many more opportunities to work and live a totally full life, and she was tired of the slow pace of the Yellowhammer State. She planned to move up to Edgewater and hopefully get a fashion design job in the Big Apple. She said she thrived on the busyness of this area, and it pushed her to do better. To each their own, but I do think some people really do well there, but for me, it was just something I was not enjoying anymore. I really was craving a more peaceful life, especially after I got PTSD after one terrible night in Atlantic City.

It was my 21st birthday weekend, and we were hitting up the clubs. It happened. I took a drink from a random man that was drugged. I do not remember much, but I then woke up in the hospital feeling a bit in pain and the doctor explained I had been assaulted. I remember crying and just feeling so overwhelmed. My boyfriend at the time, Sam, was sitting there in a chair next to me and once I woke up he came over and wrapped me in the longest hug ever.

Soon after the incident, I switched to living back at home and decided to just commute down to Monmouth University. I just needed to be with my family for the remainder of my college years. That incident was my first time I saw just how dark the world can be. A few weeks later, I started to feel different. Noises started to startle me more, and I had nightmares. It started to feel like the darkness from the assault was overtaking my well-being. My mind started to feel more horrifying, it was such an unpleasant feeling. My mom started to look for ways to help me and found a doctor who's main specialty was helping people after traumatic events. I then went to a psychiatrist and was diagnosed with the mental health disorders of Generalized Anxiety Disorder and Posttraumatic Stress Disorder. She then put me on an anti-anxiety medication Xanax. It really helped with settling my mind down.

After I graduated from college, I felt a change was necessary. All the noisiness of Jersey was just really not conducive to my healing and I felt a move might be good. I thought switching to a state that was less chaotic and more chill was what I needed. The first place that came to mind was the West Coast. I heard from a friend that had moved out there that the stereotype was true. It was more of a chill environment over there. I mean every state is probably more relaxed than New Jersey. To be honest, I now realize I was not the biggest fan of Jersey. I love to have more fun and here the environment is a lot to handle. It is a more serious and developed way of living. I remember when we did a two-week long vacation to California when I was 14 and thinking it would be such a cool place to live. The mix of cities and epic nature was just so sweet. I can party in a city or in the woods, that is so dope. Something was pulling me and letting me know it was time for a move.

While I did not end up in California, Washington has really become home. I ended up moving to the Seattle area really because that was the first place I could find a good computer programming job. I did apply to a couple of companies down in the San Francisco area but none of them got back to me. When I first arrived in Seattle, I just remembered thinking what a breath of fresh air this place is, (both literally and figuratively). For real, it is so much cleaner up here and so much less congested than Dirty Jersey. That is what I call it now. Yeah, I know that is not the nicest nickname, but sometimes it is fun to kind of trash where you are from. Not everyone is in love with their roots and I think that is completely fine.

Sometimes, part of me does miss it out there. I think it only has to do with the fact that most of my family stayed around the northeast. It can be hard not to have them nearby. It was a scary choice to move someplace where I did not know anyone, but in the long run it really paid off. Life is too short to not live in some place you are not happy with. Sometimes change can be scary but also an excellent thing to do for yourself. Thankfully, I quickly made a few friends out here. Bryce and I clicked almost instantly and then, a few months later, I joined a "Young singles in Seattle Meetup" and made a couple of other great friends from there. No matter where you are, I now truly believe you will always be able to find your tribe.

And if I did not move out here I would not have met such a wonderful man as Bryce. Our friendship is so special, and we really have such an amazing time together. Whatever woman gets him will be the luckiest one ever. He is such a great guy. Before I met him, when I moved up here, it was really lonely, but he added a light to my life I didn't even know I needed. I do not think he even fully grasps how much our friendship means to me. One of the most special things in life is finding those people who get you. I have not even told him about the assault I went through, because what would that do? I am not what happened to me, I am that fun Jersey girl who I will always be. He saw me for my true self and having at least one person who just embraces your whole being makes living life so worth it.

Chapter 12: Carly

I hopped out of the shower and put on my pajamas. After a long day, there really is no better feeling than getting freshened up and being all cozy. I then grabbed my phone and watched some Instagram Reels showing great outdoor places to visit in Oregon. I enjoyed some that show parks along the coast as well as some other forested ones more inland. I am just learning about so many new nature areas down there, and it is truly staggering how many there are. Such a magical place that state is. I take in the short reels showcasing areas of the rugged coastline and I stare at the screen in awe. The giant rocks in the ocean that I see on the video are just so jaw-dropping. It is like chunks of the mountains were ripped off and thrown into the water. The feeling of the travel content oozes the same special feeling it brings if I were down there right now. I feel transported back there for a moment through the moving images, which bring me such a sense of pure joy.

It has been a few weeks since that epic trip, and I already cannot wait to go back. There are so many other new places there we still have to explore. I told the girls we have to see some other parks and they were in total agreement. It is so nice to have friends that actually want to go on many epic adventures with me. I know not everybody has people like that. There are a lot of folks out there who are homebodies and no judgment at all to people who enjoy that. There is greatness to just relaxing too, but the travel lover in me just cannot be still. Oh, how grateful I am to have two amazing friends to experience it all with.

A few minutes after enjoying that content, I noticed a message had arrived again from Bryce. As I look down at the text I begin to imagine where we could go for their next date. I then began my reply "How about the Seattle waterfront over by the sculpture park?" That could be such a great follow-up date. I think that might be fun because it is a little more artsy. Good to change things up a bit. Like our last one was all about nature, this time let us mix a little bit of culture into our outing. In life, I feel human-induced art and nature both offer their own distinctive beauty. While in nature you get to appreciate the magic that comes all naturally from our amazing world, art is a chance to share the human experience. Whether it's paintings, sculptures, music or movies, all of them offer a chance to partake in something special people have decided to create.

A few minutes later, I got a text back, "Sure! That is an awesome idea, maybe stop somewhere for dinner after too?" I know there is a delicious sushi place right by there. It could be a great way to get to know each other more. Sitting at a table with someone is such an intimate thing. I then replied "That would be great, up for a sushi place?" I hope he is a sushi lover too, because if I am being totally honest, it may be hard to date a guy who is not. Alright, it would not be a total deal breaker per say but kind of would be a bit sad. I then put my phone down and then have an apple for a quick snack.

The next morning, I awoke, and realized I had forgotten to set my alarm. Oh crap, what time is it? I looked at my phone and saw it was 7:30 am. Oh shoot, I'm so late. I then thought I had better call my boss and let him know. "Mark, I'm so sorry I'm running late today. I will be there no later than 8:30. "It is OK, it happened. Just please be here as soon as you can." Thank God I have a chill boss. I had a feeling he would not be too mad knowing Mark, but I just felt like a fool. We are only human though, right, and this is the first time since I have been in the workforce that I ever pulled anything like this. As I get in the car and begin the commute, I remind myself of my humanity. It is so important to remember that and just accept the flaws, because at the end of the day we are all just trying to do our best. I think there is so much beauty in just embracing that and letting go. This is life, and it is not a perfect thing. It is a beautiful crazy ride that every single one of us is on.

I made my way home after an interesting Thursday. After I had my dinner and checked my phone and saw a message from Bryce, "Sushi sounds good, so how about I meet you at 3pm on Saturday near the red sculpture that kind of resembles the aliens from War of the worlds?" I chuckle and think this guy is so cute, war of the worlds hehe. I then replied "Interesting way to describe it lol love that though, 3pm sounds good." I am excited about this next date and to see where things will go next. There is a natural flow between us. That is already a good sign. If I have learned anything so far in life it is that you only want people who truly get you, to be by your side for the long haul.

Chapter 13: Together

"I always found this park so interesting", Bryce begins "This is only my second time here, but I find these sculptures really fascinating. Seattle has such a cool artsy vibe. I have always admired how creative it is up here " It really does, I feel like this city is not afraid to stand out in a strange way which, to be honest, is really cool." They continue to walk down the path full of sculptures with the sun shining its summer light upon them radiating a sense of warmth. They pass the many odd designs built by outrageously talented artists, putting them both in a sense of amusement. Even as the rush of the city is right beside them, they both feel like they are in their own little peaceful world. With the loving embrace casting a sense of safety between them.

"Do you ever miss California?" "To be honest, not really. I mean, yes, they do say there is no place like home and maybe that is partially true due to my family living there, but moving up here has been liberating. I do love the West Coast, and also it is not like I moved to Alabama, but something about the change to Washington has been magical. I don't know, I think there's just something about this area that I really love." Bryce smiles "You know, this may sound silly, but I read once from a travel page on Instagram. You go to the desert southwest region to feel free, but you can come here, the Pacific Northwest, to feel alive. Maybe it is just that you feel more alive here." Wow, that is a great way to put it, I really love that. I really agree, something about the huge evergreens and so many waterways does convey that, there is something magical about this region. It is like a mix of super cozy and rustic vibes." "It really is a special place." They both then smile at each other, realizing how natural their connection is.

"How would it be for our next date if we climbed Mount Rainier?" Bryce asks jokingly. He can sense the love she has for Washington, which he is not surprised about. Something about here makes it such a beloved place to be and for good reason. I have heard tourists say that this region of America really has such a unique vibe compared to any other states. That the extremely rustic nature and less housing development and snow capped mountains everywhere you turn is so refreshing to see.

"I think I need to do some harder hikes before I make it to that one. I know we are from the era of embracing that you only live once, but I ain't trying to kill myself." Bryce smiles, "Ah yes, the YOLO era, crazy to think, in like 10 years we went from a crazy partying time to now everyone being obsessed with self-improvement." Carly rolls her eyes, "For sure, but can we please bring back the fun times, not too sound old but everything is so goth now." "I guess we both are true to the era we grew up in," Bryce said with a radiant smile on his face.

As they finish up walking they both cannot deny the physical attraction. Eye contact and smiles keep coming out like they both just want to be so close to each other. "You are so beautiful Carly; I'm sorry if that sounds like I am coming off too strong." " It may be a little much, but I think part of me is liking it, I appreciate the lust. At least we know the attraction is there." "I still cannot believe how you have not been scooped up yet, it is wild. You are pretty much the perfect lady. Like totally flawless." Carly stops and thinks before carefully planning her philosophical response," Well, I really appreciate you saying all that but I am definitely not perfect. I really think we all have some darkness in us, even the most seemingly joyful individuals. However, I do believe I try my best to nurture the light that is in me. I think we all are just trying our best though" " I mean that is true. I have had moments where darkness seemed to be a lot, when I was little my dad got taken from us way too soon from cancer. Sorry if that was a bit too much of a trauma dump, but what I am trying to say is I understand what you are saying. We all are going to have pain thrown at us to some extent in life, but you have a choice as to what to do with it." "Bryce I am so sorry for your loss, I mean I could not imagine going through that, but look what you have become, a fantastic man and great computer programmer taking on Seattle, I am so proud of you."

Bryce thinks her words just feel so magical. He cannot help but admire how smart and loving she is. "I am sure though you have had so many guys approach you though" "I mean yes, of course, but most of the time they come off right away with very sexual remarks. I know there are great guys out there but some of you can be so horny. No offense like I get it, I enjoy sex too. I did have this one guy who did when I was out at a bar in Portland with my friends. He seemed really nice and I thought there may be potential for something bigger. After two dates though, he told me he is not really interested in a romantic connection right now and only cares to be friends with benefits." Bryce chuckled, "Typical man." "Right and to each their own, but I love enjoying life with others and view sex as part of a relationship. That is ok too. Not everyone is into hookup culture ya know? I would like to have a man to do more than just the deed with."

"I think humans get scared to get close to someone else, which is why now with dating apps it is so much easier to find quick fun." "Right, but I feel deep connections and having that one person to love can make life even more magical, don't people want someone to share all the beauty of this world with, I mean I have not even had a serious relationships yet but from what I heard from others love can be a special thing" That quote got Bryce thinking about how he wants true love. How he is not a guy into quick hookups, that is his content with his beautiful life and wants someone who will help enhance it. He wants someone who he can be there for in the hard times and they can be there for him. This rings especially true to him since he knows how hard pain can be sometimes. Once he and the right lady come together, he will do his best to sincerely never hurt her. He then replies "It is even hard for me, I feel like I'm too much of a gentleman and some women actually more of a bad guy, for us good guys looking for a special lady it can be so hard too."

They walk into the sushi restaurant and it is packed, which is no surprise as it is one of the best ones in the city. With the smooth electronic music playing in the background, the place has such a chic vibe. They end up waiting about 20 minutes before getting a small table close to the bar. The restaurant is full of people having a great time just enjoying the city life out on a great night. Whether it is a couple seeming to have a date night, or family having a sweet outing, everyone seems to be living their best life enjoying the fresh and seemingly delicious food . They decide to order a few different kinds of rolls to share. Eel avocado, shrimp tempura, spicy tuna, and a California one arrive at their table. "God that looks so delicious," Carly says.

They dive into the plate, wasting no time, and devour every piece of the amazing sushi. "That was so tasty," Bryce says. They both grin at each other just enjoying this moment. "So how's work been?" He says. "It has been, ok, a little while ago there was this whole fiasco with stuff getting leaked from Amazon's server and that was probably one of the most stressful weeks of my life, and the people from Amazon just can be so uptight so when something goes wrong while working with them, it can be hell." " That sounds terrible, I actually have not worked on any projects for them yet, but I know how our clients can sometimes get." "Yes definitely, I heard about how they treated one of the managers and I thought to myself, can I give them some weed?" "Yeah, well I guess money can make people crazy, I personally just want to work to be able to live safely and do fun things." "For sure, I think if more people worked to live and not lived to work, there would be a bit more happiness in our world."

As they get ready to head home, they both feel a sense of pure joy from such a beautiful night. The Seattle city lights illuminate the scene behind them as they walk out of the restaurant. The skyscrapers surround them as they stand face to face with one another on the busy street. "Thank you again for such a fun time Bryce, I really hope we can do this more. "Thank you as well, I had a blast." They both hug and want the feeling to stay. They allow it to linger for about twenty seconds before going in for a kiss. It was a gentle, sweet one, nothing too sensual, but from that kiss they both started to see the sparks between them flying high like the heights of the Cascade Mountains. The journey is just getting started, and who knows where it will take them? Just like the wide free landscapes of the Pacific Northwest, they know there could be so much beauty to be found in their sweet little connection.

Chapter 14: Bryce

The office phone at Bryce's desk rings, he picks it up. "Bryce here." " Hey Bryce, this is Mark, whenever you have a free moment can you please come to my office?" "Alright sir, no worries, I will be there in a bit." Mark is really a cool boss. In the few years I have worked here, he really has never gotten mad at me. There was even a time he probably should have, but he still let it slide. During the first year I started working, on break, I decided to watch some YouTube videos on my desk computer. Our company has a policy that states no websites for personal use should ever be used. It could even result in immediate termination, I was told by HR during training. I was young and was like, well how will they find out? Plus, it is not like I'm doing anything bad. I just wanted to check out a quick one about this top tier trail down at Zion National Park.

Well, to my surprise, they can view every website and program we use each day. I ended up getting caught, but all Mark said was please do not do that again. He did not even sound angry and that was such a surprise given what I was thinking probably would happen. So right now I am wondering what he is calling me in the office for today. He never micromanages us and that incident which happened almost five years ago was the last time I had a one on one office chat with him. Overall I feel more intrigued than nervous to figure out what is going on.

After lunch, I make it down to his office feeling a bit of anxiety as I enter the room. "Hey Bryce, come on in," He says. "Is everything ok?" He then replies "Yes, I will be straight up honest now there is nothing to be nervous about, this is not a disciplinary meeting." My nerves then fade away, and I feel such a sense of gratitude for him saying that already. "So Bryce, I'm sure you may have heard that back in April we opened our second office in Billings." I pause for a moment trying to remember, "Oh yes actually I do recall seeing the email about that." "Awesome, well, first I want you to know we truly appreciate all your work and also how kind you are to our clients. You are an outstanding addition to the team here at Seaside" I think I have a feeling I know where this is going. "Well of course, thank you for providing a great work environment, honestly I know not all companies have such a healthy one." "Alright, second this is a straight up offer, but we want to let you know, we want to give you the chance to take on a supervising role over there with a huge pay raise, I'm going to hand you the terms and conditions written here on these papers but you have two weeks to let me know if you want to lock in with it and take the new position. If you are going to accept, I will just need your signature on the last page handed in by the due date"

Bryce takes the papers from Mark and walks out of his office. So many thoughts are running through my mind. Promotion. Raise. Montana. A sense of excitement fills my spirit but also one of confusion. Washington is pretty much all I have known. I have friends here and l love this state. But a new supervisor position sounds like it could bring a lot of good. I never really cared about promotions. My motto has been to work to live not live to work. I always did my best but it was never a dream to be in a higher company role. Mark really sees me fit for this position though which in a way is gratifying. I then looked down at the paper as I was standing in the hallway and found the salary. I cannot believe my eyes when I see it, they are offering me a whopping $175,000. Wow. That is like $65,000 more than I'm making now. It sounds amazing. Also, Montana is such a beautiful place. I have done a few trips out there seeing some of their parks and such it is a special place. It is even more rural than Washington, which is nice, and I have heard Billings is a beautiful small city. It sounds great, but I really need to let this all sink in. I still have two weeks before a final decision is needed. Oh, and then there is one other setback to all this, Carly. I know we have only had two dates, but there is no denying we already have a special connection. I am not a true believer in love at first sight, but I do think some people just hit it off naturally and that is definitely the truth for us. All I can do, I guess, is take it day by day, but sometimes the future we have coming up can make that so hard.

"You are telling me they are offering you a $50,000 dollar raise and a better position and all you have to do is move two states over?! I would do that in a heartbeat!" Crystal says loudly through my IPhone with her Jersey accent blaring towards my ears. When I got home, I knew I needed to call her and discuss this jarring news. " "I know it does not sound so bad, but it really is a big decision to make." "There is no decision to be made, you take that!" Crystal is way more daring than me, I mean moving from one coast to the other all alone is not something everyone could do. "And also, who knows who you will meet out there, look I met you an amazing friend a whole 3,000 miles away from my hometown. Just imagine if I never did the move we most likely would not be talking right now ""But here is the other thing, I recently met a nice girl here who seems special." "You just started talking and getting to know each other, people cannot be trusted especially in today's age! You know how many options people have now for finding someone? Literally everyone's in a throuple now it seems. She may turn on you to join one herself for all you know " I laugh at the second part of her comment. I do not know if that many people are actually in a relationship with more than one person. However, there is a lot of truth to what she is saying. Life can really surprise you sometimes. I think back to my college years and how many unexpected, special things came along through so many great people I met. I had a few really great friends who I will remember for my whole life. Yeah, I do not interact much with a lot of them anymore besides some Facebook reactions, but the point is, new environments can allow you to meet amazing people. Sometimes, too, I think change could be good. I mean Montana is such a beautiful state as well. Crystal seems right. This should be a no-brainer, but for some reason my soul is making this a conflict. This is really a decision that I wish I had longer than two weeks to make.

Once I get off the phone, my mind continues to race. I decide to hop over to the den and find something to watch on Netflix. Right as I was about to start the show, I heard a ding come from my phone. I see there is a new text from Carly. "Hey handsome, when can I see you again? ;)" I set my phone down feeling so torn. The emotion of confusion began to fill myself like a wave growing to its peak in the ocean. Life can be so consuming at times. Here I am with a beautiful sweet woman who we already have a special connection with and, at the same time, I am thrown by this curveball. I did not reply. I set my phone down and hit the play button, trying to use the show as a distraction from this big decision I am being forced to make.

Chapter 15: Mark

My job sometimes seems to be greater than just tedious work. In moments where I am able to give an outstanding worker a promotion, I am reminded that there is good and bad intertwined in everything. It is a nice gesture to be able to help someone climb the ladder which can lead to a more fulfilling life. I think one of my favorite parts of being here is seeing newer employees thrive.

Here at Seaside Programming we are a for-profit entity trying to make the most funds possible. I will say to everyone that is why we exist. Business does serve society, but at the end of the day, making money is our goal. My CEO even tells me, "Find the most work to get done at the most you can get them to pay is our main motto." So I totally get the point of all this. But, a lot of good things about my days here stem from the fact that I am still a human with three kids of my own and a beautiful wife. I do care about others. I like to think of myself as a pretty nice guy. Getting to offer a young, smart and capable young man a higher-paying job is something special. It can provide an opportunity to give himself a life in which he can really live it to the maximum potential.

It brought so many smiles to all of my kids' faces when we were able to take a trip to Vermont last fall. My wife had really wanted to visit and my oldest son, Jackson, really did too. He is 13 now and really is starting to appreciate traveling. He had never been up to New England either and was excited about heading out east for the first time. It seemed like it would be the perfect fall getaway. Here out west, because of the species of trees we mainly have, foliage is not as common. So it was going to be really exciting to have such an immersive autumn experience. Even though I have been out east, I had never, at the time, been to Vermont yet either. For years though, I have seen pictures of it and it always looked gorgeous. With the many small towns surrounded by colorful leaves, rolling hills and pumpkins. It always seemed to be the perfect state to visit if you want the best fall vibes.

We were able to spend a week and a half in a rustic cabin surrounded by gold, orange and red foliage everywhere. The forest had an overbearing sense of beauty. Even though the mountains were much smaller up there, bigger is not always better. I now know because the hills and forests there all created the perfect autumn experience. Drinking the warm fresh apple cider while climbing up the hills hiking in Green Mountain National Forest was another moment I will always cherish. Seeing my three little ones with smiles filling their faces during that vacation was such an amazing memory we were able to create. I know, though, none of that would have been possible without money.

Then there was one day this past spring. I just surprised each of my kids with their first iPad. I know it is just a material thing. That one day it would all fade to dust and be worth nothing, but at that moment, the excitement they showed felt like the most precious thing in the universe. That same night, I was feeling extra generous and I even treated them to dinner at the Rainforest Café. They adored seeing all the animatronic animals come to life as they enjoyed their delicious food. I remember my youngest one, Allison, being so gleeful when the monkeys started to move. I then let them all pick a souvenir stuffed animal from the gift shop. On the car ride home they all looked so joyful. Even Jackson, now officially a teenager, was still joining in on the fun. What a beautiful day that was. The flowers were blooming everywhere too, and now gloomy clouds were in the sky. Spring was really beginning to fully blossom. It was just a sunny day at a perfect high temperature of 70 degrees. It showed me that some of the most simple moments can add the most precious value to life.

I am blessed to have a supervisor role. It is a lot less stressful of a position in some ways. I have worked my way through from the bottom up, so I know how rewarding it can be to finally achieve a great level of success. Something about giving this offer to Bryce feels great too. He is a worker who takes pride in doing a good job. We have quite a few employees who, you can tell, all do the bare minimum. Nothing against that too. I understand most people have no choice but to work to survive. It is nice though, when a man like him gives it his all. Every day, you can see it. How his life means something more to him.

I am not sure if in the end he will officially take the offer, but I can say that this could possibly be a way for him to better his life. A chance for a new start and a great salary that could give him new possibilities he did not have before. It is his life though, and at the end of the day I am just his boss, but laying the offer out there for him made my day have a bit of an extra touch of joy.

I also understand that moving to another state can be a hard decision to make. I know that all too well, actually. When I was a young boy in middle school, living near Salt Lake City, my parents lost their steak house. They had been in operation for almost 20 years, but the region was starting to see more development. More development means more businesses and more business means more competition. I am going to sound ancient saying this, but I kind of miss the good old days. A lot of things are becoming more and more corporate now and life has gotten really fast-paced. It was kind of sad to see all the massive construction that came to the area. More people were opening restaurants, especially other steakhouses. Out west, especially in states like Utah and Colorado, cattle are abundant. It is a big staple of food in those states. That meant for my family's restaurant it would be harder to stay alive.

A few weeks after the unfortunate closing, a sort of miracle and curse had happened. My dad's old buddy who moved to Massachusetts years ago said he is looking to give up his pizza shop near Boston. He presented my family with a great opportunity, and they took that in a heartbeat. Restaurant ownership was their passion. However, that left me as a young boy to really struggle with the big move. Once we made the transition, it was really hard to adjust. For one, I had left all my friends behind for a totally different region of the country. It really almost felt like moving from living in a small hut on a palm-filled beach in Hawaii to a townhouse on a busy street in Brooklyn. It was so different up there. The landscapes, the food, and the people all felt so foreign. It was almost like I was on a different planet. I really missed it out west. The north-east just was not for me. I truly could not wait to one day go back to the wide open spaces of the west. I was longing for the day in which I would leave the hustle and bustle of the congested southern New England area.

Well, one thing I learned for sure so far in my 47 years on this planet is things always work out the way they should. If something is really meant to be, it will happen. Either we will make it come to be or the choice will be made for us by something bigger. I know now that I am happy with the way life has turned out. I have an amazing family and a great job and live somewhere I truly love. It may take time, but the right things for our lives always end up falling into place. I am a big believer that our souls all have their unique destiny and everything we face, from the worst situations to the most amazing ones, all make up what it means to live a true, full life.

Chapter 15: Carly

It was around 1:30 on a Wednesday afternoon and the Seaside Programming office was in a more quiet state. It being not super busy allowed my mind to drift off more often than usual to Bryce. It had been a few days since our last date, and I was so ready to see him again. I noticed though he didn't text me back last night. I know people get busy, but usually by now I would have heard from him. I hope he is doing alright. I get out of my desk for a second to head over to the break room. I feel like I need a glass of water. I walked over there and as I made my way in, noticed a man sitting down eating a sandwich. A man who I happen to know pretty well. "Hello there Bryce." I noticed his face looking surprised, like he definitely was not expecting this. "Uhhh Hey Carly, what's good?" I walked over towards him, deciding to take a seat, noticing his nerves. "All good, funny to see you here, so the other floors they have do not have a break room? I have not been over there much." "They do, actually. I just like coming to this one for a little change of scenery. And I get to stretch my legs a bit more because of the walk." I pause before going on then staring him deep in the eyes, "I had so much fun this weekend with you, want to do it again soon?" He does not respond right away and something looks different about him. Bryce seems off today. I can tell he is carrying something heavy. He pauses before letting out and sighing, "Carly there is something I need to tell you." I know that buddy. Your facial expressions and body language give that all away. " Go ahead, I am here for you." "I really love spending time with you and I sense there really could be something special between us." "I do too, so what's going on then?" "I was offered a supervisor position for the company's new office in Montana and I don't know what to do." My eyes turn sympathetic.Then a sense of melancholic energy fills the room. I know the struggles work can bring to life. I mean look at me, I had to move 1,000 miles away from home for the job. The thing, though, was I had just graduated from college and was so free. I guess change can come at any time. Like how the sun sets and rises each day, life can be that way too. In one moment it all can seem like you are heading in one direction and then boom, your life gets the biggest curve ball thrown at you that it has ever seen.

Back home, I did not have a stunning man there who I was attracted to. I could imagine though, if I did, it would make a life decision much harder. "I mean this is your life Bryce, but I want you to know that as long as you stay here, and as long as you want to get to know me, I am willing. Also, I would not be opposed to long distance if things with us did progress well." "Long distance Carly? Really? What are we in high school? That is such a dumb idea." "Hey I am just trying to help, no need to get angry!" She exclaims. "No need to get angry? Carly, do you know why I am so upset right now? It is because I have never felt like this about anyone before. And right when I meet a woman who is as amazing as you after never having a connection like this in my 27 years of living, the universe decides to throw me this amazing job promotion? This is complete bull shit." I then saw Bryce rise up and slam his chair in and then storm towards the door. "Bryce!" I yelled "Stop! Let's be like grown-ups and talk about the damn thing!" "There is nothing to talk about Carly, I just can't...." Then tears begin to spill from his eyes. " I just don't know what to do." Carly then puts her arms around him in the tightest hug she has ever given someone before. "It is ok, I'm guessing you don't have to decide this right now, just be here with me at this moment " "I have less than two weeks" he says in a muffled voice. They hug and the tears in Bryce's eyes begin to subside. "It is OK, I will give you some space," Carly says. I backed away from him while still holding some sweet eye contact. I do not want to upset him any further. Everyone needs some space sometimes. Then we both begin the walks back to our desks. I never expected something like that to happen. Never, especially in the middle of a work day in the break room. I feel like this is one of the first overly emotional experiences I have had so far. Something about that makes my heart skip a few beats. Life definitely is not all sunshine and rainbows, and while I have dealt with some challenges in the past, I think right now this one may be the most heartrending.

When I got in my car I decided it would be helpful to give Britney a call. Her more honest and slightly cynical outlook on life is so vital in situations like these. "Wow, well I'm really sorry this all happened." "It's fine, I reply, it is just such a frustrating situation, like the stars are aligning for me and him and this gets thrown into the mix. It's just I have never had this organic and special connection with anyone before." I replied. "Well, Carly, if you both really feel this way, then I believe it is worth fighting for. I mean genuine bonds like what you say it is with Bryce are rare. Especially in today's age, I mean you know how easy it is for people to find sex on the apps now." "I know it really is, I just don't want to be the reason he stops living a full life, and I can't just move to Montana with him. There are barely any programming jobs out there. And what would I do without you and Sara? I would be heartbroken without seeing you as much."I then hung up with Britney and a thought ran through my mind. I know exactly what I have to do.

When I pull up to my driveway, I decide to text Bryce. "Hey, I know I said I would leave you alone, but do you want to hang out at my place on Friday evening after work? It's just to talk and spend some time together. No pressure if you don't want to :)." I then headed inside and had some dinner. I then decided to listen to some music. Some magic coming into my headphones sounds perfect right now.

After such an emotional and unexpectedly crazy day, some self care time is needed. I hopped on to Spotify and pressed play to one of my favorite albums ever, Teenage Dream by the queen Katy Perry. All the songs are pop perfection from the golden age of the 2010s party music era. It is such a great escape and I have come to learn that when I have a rough day, this album almost immediately brings a smile to my face.

Jam after jam the album plays through, bringing such a euphoric feeling to my soul. Once the song Hummingbird Heartbeat comes on, it is like all the pain from today has been wiped away. Music is such a gift. How it can bring the beauty it does really is something spiritual. The final song plays but the glee still fills me up. Then a few minutes later after I had taken my airpods out, a message notification came in. It is an IMessage from Bryce.

"Sure Carly, that actually seems like it could be really nice, I can be there around 7. That sound good?" A sense of relief fills my spirit. I just think us spending some time together in my cozy home can help sort things out and make us really see what should come next. Also, it is just nice to have some actual one on one human connection, living alone has its perks, but it can get lonely sometimes .That is perfect. Cannot wait. Oh, and by the way, do you like tacos? Was wanting to cook us a nice meal if that is OK?" A minute later, the three typing dots start going and the reply from Bryce comes through, "love tacos, I bet they will be delicious. Can't wait." "Have a good night". I then text out and sent, "You too Carly."

Chapter 16: Bryce

After work, I just feel so glad that Friday is here. Sometimes the happiness the end of the week brings can feel like the first drop of a towering roller coaster. A mix of joy and some relief that the hard part is over. The roller coaster this time feels so satisfying. The week was crazy, and I am so ready for a chill couple of days. It is so wild how much can change in your life in just a matter of a few moments. These past couple of days have really felt like a few months. Although seeing life can change quickly is nothing new to me, so I feel like I am a bit more prepared for the bumps of life. I remember that after only 3 months of my dad's cancer diagnosis, he was gone forever. From the news about the job promotion to the discussion with Carly, it has been a lot to take in. I am still excited about seeing her tonight. Just getting to be at her home, have a nice meal and talk things out sounds really like a fantastic idea. I know deep down that going on adventures which I love to do is so amazing, but there really is something special to being in the comfort of a home, especially now I realize that having this beautiful woman in my life.

I pull up to Carly's apartment feeling a little nervous. I have not spent one on one time in a living space with someone since senior year of high school. To be honest, that was my last relationship. Lia was a beautiful and nice one, but she ended it with me literally a few days before we graduated. Her reason was that she was going to a different school in the fall and wanted the freedom to explore herself more. Fair enough. I mean I did really like her. However, I always did have a small gut feeling that maybe it was not going to last forever. We still keep in touch from time to time and we did have some great experiences together. We went surfing together and those are some of the most fun memories I have of my high school years. It is always good to revisit those exciting times in my head once in a while. Just remembering the freedom we felt while surfing along the coast is such a beautiful feeling.

Thinking about Lia got me really pondering about all the what if's in life. Like I wondered for a moment what that could have looked like. Would I be a dad already and we would have a house building a life for our family? Would it even have worked out to get to that point or was the connection with Lia all doomed from the get go. Was everything already predetermined for us? All these thoughts pulled me back to what is going on with Carly now and being thrown the promotion offer. Could this already be predestined to be a temporary thing or is the really the women

"Hey Bryce, come on in" Carly says as she opens her front door. "Thank you so much for inviting me over tonight." As I enter, I notice how beautiful her apartment is decorated. With gorgeous nature artwork of the Redwoods on the wall and vanilla candles burning, her home has such a special energy running through it. I took off my shoes then stared up at her beautiful self. It was not even just about her looks I have come to realize, she was always so smiley too and that was able to enhance the joy I felt, or help me feel better when things were rough. We then walked over to her kitchen table where there were tortilla chips lying out as well as some homemade guacamole. I just think about how much care she put into this night and how happy I am for this moment we are about to share. "Can I get you a bud light lime or, do I also have some sweet wine coolers if you are more of a fruity drink kind of guy?" I smile, "Did I ever give an impression that I enjoyed those kinds of drinks to you, something about the way that question is framed makes me think I did?" She looks deeply in my eyes before going on "Well Bryce, you are the most sensitive and sweet man I have met so yeah you kind of did." "Well, your thoughts proved right, I will take the blue raspberry one if you can?" "Only cherry or passion fruit left", "Well passion fruit it is then" I reply.

The taco shells, flour tortillas, chicken and toppings are all brought out onto the table looking like a Cinco de Mayo festival. My mouth begins to water as the essence of the Mexican spiced chicken begins to fill up the dining room in an all-consuming way. "Carly, this might be the nicest thing someone has ever done for me, thank you for all of this." We begin to create our tacos and start to munch away. I opted for the crunchy shell as Carly went for a soft one. "So what have you been up to lately?" she asks. "Well, the honest answer is not much besides work and then,. Overthinking about what I am going to do with this promotion offer." She then stops eating for a second before I can tell she is carefully planning her answer, "I want you to know, as I said before, this is completely your decision, but I also need you to realize,

I personally feel we have a beautiful connection and if you want to stay and see where this goes I would be extremely happy. But let's not try to talk or think about this much tonight, I just want to enjoy our time now." Her answer brings a sense of peace. She is right. I should just push that aside for now. It is not every night I have a beautiful and kind person cook a stunning taco fiesta for us to enjoy.

We then moved over to the couch and decided to pop on a movie. "If this is too cheesy, we do not have to do it, but I saw The Notebook is streaming on Netflix and was thinking it would be cute to watch together." I cannot help but to smile, "That is fine, I would watch The Emoji Movie with you if you wanted." She laughs "Ok, but seriously it was not that bad, like was it a 90s Disney masterpiece? Not even close, but for mindless, colorful animated fun, it was ok." "Alright Carly now you are going to make me question if our connection is actually genuine." I playfully teased her. "Hey to each their own I guess. Art is so subjective ""Yeah I mean I really loved The Kissing Booth films and those were no cinematic masterpieces." Carly chuckles so loud, "Oh my god, you would love those, why am I not surprised at all about this?" "Hey they're really cute and besides chick flick is actually a man made construct, guys should love whatever they are drawn to. We should not be put in a box to watch just Marvel, DC and Fast and The Furious movies."

Before I know it, The Notebook is about thirty minutes in, and Carly and I are cuddling in such a sappy manner. Her head is down on my chest while my arms are tight around her. The comfort of us being curled next to each feels like drinking a warm hot chocolate on a cozy fall day somewhere in the colorful foliage of New Hampshire. The energy between us has a heartfelt sweetness that I have never prior experienced when being next to a woman. The loving nature between Ally and Noah on the screen is beautiful to watch but our time together feels like our own real life version of that. "They are literally the cutest" Carly whispers in my ears. "I love it, this is actually my first time seeing it." "You have never seen The Notebook before? Oh my god, how?!" "I know, it is crazy! It is so iconic from what I have heard. I always wanted to though and last year I was actually looking on Netflix for it. Was not there yet " That's streaming for you. You never know when something you want will be put up or taken down. It is literally like the best movie though." "It is so good, especially watching it here with you makes it even more beautiful." I replied. The movie then finishes up and tears fill our eyes. "I did not expect it to end so sad, but there was something cathartic about it." It got me thinking too. We do not get many romantic movies like that anymore, especially on the big screen. I am not sure what the exact reasoning is but I wish we had more sweet romance movies now in the 2020's. What a touching masterpiece that film is.

Carly then starts kissing me gently and I feel a tension between us. "Let's head over to the bedroom now." We walk offer there with our hands clasped together in the sweetest way possible. We get to the bed and take our shirts off and a few minutes later we begin to make love. In the most gentle way possible I begin thrusting and the beautiful connection we have found in just a few weeks feels like a powerful burst of electricity now. Our breathing speeds up with each movement as we fully become one with each other with our bodies merging. The sweetness of her hands rubbing my shoulders feels almost too magical. It feels so natural the way we are touching each other and brings a supernatural romantic closeness that I have never felt. We finish and I give her a kiss on the forehand. It does not feel anything close to the couple hookups I did in college. It does not even feel like it did when Lia and I made love. There is a true feeling of comfort and safety that came from us having sex "Just lay with me here now, just be here Bryce, you are a special man." We then lay side by side with my arms clasped against her. A silence fills the room with the dark skies outside, but somehow right here with us together, creates the brightest light I have ever felt even while covered in full darkness.

I decide to spend the night there and something about it feels utterly magical. Carly ends up falling asleep before me and as I lay there with her beautiful self beside me, my mind begins to ruminate. Thoughts about the job transfer begin to plague me and consume my being. Do I really want to leave this all behind for a higher position and better pay? Part of me does feel compelled to move to Montana though, a new state could be exciting. My brain feels like it is in the middle of one of the worst tug of war battles ever. I decide it is best to put on some relaxing sleep music and take out my air pods. That will allow the peaceful sounds to permeate deep into my body. I need to get some rest, and I remind myself that I know the universe will guide me to the right decision. Even if whatever it will be is going to be coming up in less than two weeks.

<u>Chapter 17: Carly</u>

"You got the D?!" Sara exclaims through my bluetooth speaker as I am heading home from work. Her sense of enthusiasm is so sweet but it comes off as a little goofy. I think back to last night and how it was so much more than just a steamy sexual encounter. Do not get me wrong, it was really good but it was so much more special than just a quick sloppy hook up. "I sure did, it was so fun and not just the sex but the whole night. But he was an amazing love maker too, not going to lie." "It does sound quite awesome. I really am glad you guys had so much fun. You deserve it Carly" "Yeah, but I cannot get too attached because I do not know what his choice will be. If anything though, some bonding time with him did feel beautiful." "Well, just take it day by day then, what does that song say we love, if it's meant to be it will be." She sings that part to me, and she actually has a beautiful voice." "When are you going to go on American Idol?! No, but in all seriousness, I love that song, I love your voice and I love who you are. You are right about just taking it one moment at a time. Thank you. "What are best friends here for, she replied?" Shortly after that, I then hung up the call and felt the cool summer breeze come through my windows as I was driving along the interstate. It really was a special night. At this point, I do not think there is any denying this connection. It feels so genuine, but is fate more powerful than our own choices? I feel like it is one of the mysteries of life. Like, how much power do we really have over things? All I can do now is let go. Just let everything be sort of like how the water flows from the mountains of so many of the towering peaks throughout our state. All I can do is be me and allow nature to take its course. What Bryce ends up doing is out of my hands. I know deep down I have shown him exactly the person I am. I have opened myself up in a way I never had with a man before. I did everything I could, and I am proud of myself. It is not easy to be so vulnerable with someone else and if things do not work out, I can take away from this experience that there still is beauty in opening yourself up to another human.

Shortly after having some dinner, I noticed a text from Bryce.

"Thank you for last night, Carly, and thank you for all you have done."

I squinted my eyes trying to pull out what that really meant. It sounds almost like a goodbye to me. I cannot be certain though, and sometimes texts can be misconstrued.

"Of course, hey you busy Sunday, I was thinking we could maybe go kayaking on a lake?"

As the night progressed, I heard nothing from him. The silence feels like a layer of darkness because his texts always bring a smile to my face. As I am about to hit the hay, I check my phone one last time if there is a message there. It has been five hours since I sent it and still nothing.

The next day, as I headed into the office, I tried my best to brush off any thoughts of Bryce that came through my mind. Who knew that having someone ghost you after just a few weeks of talking could leave such a sting? As I pull into the parking lot and grab my purse, I feel so eager to be at work now to distract myself from this mess. Once I get out of my car and start walking, I notice a man moving past me in a fast way. Looking like he is in such a frantic rush. That man happens to be the one who just ghosted me last night. "Hey Bryce, are you trying to avoid me?" She then turns around, "Oh snap hey Carly did not even notice you, I was supposed to come in a little earlier today but was running behind." I then gaze at him. "Alright then, so you know I am still human right? If you want to ghost me, that is completely up to you, but now that we cannot disconnect so easily, and you are here right in front of me, we should talk about this." My voice is semi-stern but really not too upset. At the end of the day, people are people and if someone chooses not to be in my life, letting them go is the bravest thing you can do. "Carly, I cannot do this right now, I am already running late." "Bryce, I just want an answer, either you will choose to move or build a life with me but all this tip toeing around your decision is not good for anyone, including yourself." He begins to walk away trying to rush up to his office and disappear out of my sight. I then began to get more emotional. "It is your life, but you have brought me into it now, and I have a life too. So either stay here or move, but do not keep leaving me hanging because I know there is something beautiful between us." He then keeps walking and tears begin to spill from my eyes. I didn't even know this part of me existed. This is not my fun carefree self. I guess though true love has the ability to make anyone crazy, and right now I am living proof of that.

Once I get home and am all alone, my mind starts to race with thoughts like the fastest car going around a NASCAR track on a warm day in Southern California. The thing that is the most painful about all this, is not having an official answer. I understand he is probably still deciding, but I am pretty sure we are down to a week. He has just around seven days to make his decision. That's it. The clock is ticking.

In such a short amount of time, this could be the start of something amazing for the two of us, or it will be an incredible upgrade to his life. Like if he is going to take it, I can just let go. Just be back to enjoying fun times with Britney and Sara out in the world and hey who knows, maybe even meet a guy in person, but all this anticipation stinks. I just want to know, but right now I do not and maybe sometimes not knowing the future is better.

Chapter 18: Sara

Some might think that my fun, carefree nature is a product of an easy life and maybe there is some truth to that. I did not have any major serious family traumas during my early childhood and teen years. I was also blessed with two amazing, caring and hardworking Seattle dads. Let me tell you, growing up with two gay dads was awesome. I truly understand love is love now because they probably have one of the most pure and compassionate relationships ever. I never saw them fight, yet alone even raise their voices to one another. Sure they may have had disagreements but they always handled challenges that came about in such a healthy manner. They own and still, to this day, operate one of Seattle's longest running gay bars. When I was three years old they followed their dream and started the business and ever since then it has been a booming one. The bar was a true testament of their actual personalities because they know how to live it up. They knew how to have fun, but they were also the best family men you could ask for.

When we went on vacation they always found the most exciting things for us to do. We took a trip to southern California when I was 13 and that was one of the best weeks and half of my life. Still to this day, I do not know if I will ever be able to take a vacation that will be as exciting as that was. From all the movie studio tours to enjoying the beach and pier at Santa Monica, oh man, that was exhilarating. They found the best restaurants around Los Angeles for us to eat at and made sure to find all the best activities. We ate at this sushi restaurant called

Shining Lights Asian House and still, to this day, don't think I will ever find a cooler one. It had a really awesome celebrity theme, but there also was this huge glass window with stunning views of the ocean and palm trees. They had a rooftop with lots of plants and an even better view of the surrounding area. We also did a full day at Disneyland. It was my first time there, and I will never forget the feeling of meeting the characters. My dad knew I really wanted to meet Mater from Cars so they made sure I got a picture with him. It put such a big smile on my face. I look so corny but cute in that photo. We also visited so many beautiful parks. I will never forget the day we visited Joshua Tree National Park. Those cute trees really looked like something out of a Doctor Seuss book. Not to mention the desert scenery over there was so picturesque. It was definitely a once in a lifetime experience I will always hold near to my heart.

Their lively personalities also added such an extra level of fun to that trip. They make every place we stopped at feel extra special. They never had any worries or saw things from a cynical perspective. I think how they both modeled such bravery and fearlessness in fully embracing who they were really helped me to become the carefree and happy woman I am. We always had a good time at whatever we did while I was growing up, and I have always been a fun girl. Even in some of the times when my dads may have disagreed or were dealing with some challenges, they never allowed negativity to consume them. That does not mean I did not struggle. I have come to learn that every human has gone through at least one hard event in life, and I definitely believe that to be so true now. When I was 18, just at the brink of being able to start having my own adult life, I went through something so scary that it will stick with me for the rest of my life.

I will never forget the night of prom. It was going like every other great day and the excitement I was feeling was everywhere. Earlier that morning, I was texting with my boyfriend, Billy, and we were sharing our joy about everything great that had been going on throughout the end of this school year. A few weeks prior, we had just gotten back from our senior trip to San Francisco. It was such a pleasurable few days, and it also offered us a taste of the freedom that will come into our adult years. With the Golden Gate Bridge and Santa Cruz Mountains in the background, California was such a perfect place to have our first true trip without any parental supervision. They do not call it the golden coast for nothing and the feeling it evoked was like drinking the perfect glass of lemonade on a sunny but not too hot of a day. Beautiful, refreshing and freeing. I could never have expected how big of a curve my life would make in about a month's time.

Billy and I started dating around the beginning of 8th grade and I swore he was my forever man. We met one day when I was out riding my bike. He was pretty much the boy next door, living only three houses down from me. I have noticed him since around I was in fourth grade and always thought he was just so cute. I decided to talk to him one sunny summer day a few weeks before we were going to start our last year of middle school and from that moment we were inseparable.

We became like peanut butter and jelly that day, enjoying the warm weather and having fun in those few weeks we had left until we would be back to being at our desks. That end of the summer was another one of the best times of my life. Laughing and smiling with the evergreen trees surrounding, it was a freeing and truly joyful summer here in the pacific northwest. Young love really is so pure and carefree, maybe just for me, because I had no idea earlier that summer was when Billy started to struggle with clinical depression. His mom struggled badly with that disease as well. The brain is such an interesting part of our bodies. It is quite scary too how just having a bit of a different chemical balance can cause such darkness.

At around 4pm that prom night, I started to hear sirens near our development. For a moment I thought nothing of it, but soon they started to get closer and closer until, before I knew it, they were stopping on my street.

I looked over and could not believe my eyes, two police cars and an ambulance were surrounding Billy's house. I felt an eerie gut feeling that was letting me know something bad was going on. I told my dad about it and rushed over there. I remember scrambling by his door and frantically asking the cop what was happening. He told me in a calm but assertive manner I had to stand back, and I then immediately let him know I was Billy's girlfriend.

I was confused and worried. I had no idea about anything and it felt like an actual nightmare. There has never been a scene like this on my street in all the 18 years I have been there. A moment later, Billy was coming out on the stretcher. I frantically yelled saying what was happening and tried running towards him but before I knew it my dad was pulling me back. There I sat on the grass crying. Now it was obvious Billy was hurt, and I knew nothing at all what he went through.

A few minutes later, one cop informed me that Billy had committed a suicide. He was not going to make it as his heart rate had stopped before the ambulance arrived. They said he must have taken the bottle of his depression medication earlier in the morning as his parents were at work, so there was no way anyone could do anything to help. I sat there on the grass, in my blue prom dress weeping. I had never had so many tears come gushing out of my eyes. It was like a waterfall in its most powerful state. Water is just flowing so uncontrollably. It literally felt like someone had come and ripped my heart out of my chest. How could someone who I love so dearly be taken from me in an instant? There were pretty much no signs, and it was clear he had been suffering in silence.

Feeling completely speechless at an utter loss for words. In a moment, my pretty much perfect life was turned upside down. The love of my life is gone. At that moment, though, I knew I had a choice to make. Something bigger was telling me that, yes, I would have to grieve, but I can either turn cynical or allow this pain to remind me to never let darkness take over. I then remember thinking I wish I could have made Billy see how much he was loved, but in the end you can only save yourself. I did everything I could and we shared such a beautiful love. I was always there for him and did my best to be a loving girlfriend. I did all I could and unfortunately what happened had nothing to do with me, but now a special love was gone and cut off way too shorter than it had to be.

For the next few days, a sense of darkness was upon me. It felt like a storm cloud was consuming my whole being and the sunshine would never come back. I had never felt anything like it before. It was like the 18 years my parents instilled in me of positive vibes was being sucked away. Like a brand new vacuum pulling away all the dirt. Expect I did not want all the goodness to be taken out. After Billy's funeral around a week later, my dad had let me know we were taking a trip to Hawaii. This time we were going to stay in Maui for a week and it would be special. We had not been to that island yet, only Oahu and Kauai so far. They knewI needed to get out of the house and, with everything going on, it would be a nice respite. For a moment, I almost said no. Part of me was trying to resist and was wanting to just stay locked away in my bedroom. Not too long later though, something shifted in me and I was like no way can I pull out of this. I am not going to stop this tragedy from allowing me to move on with my life. Billy will always be in my heart and this adversity will have a lasting impact, but I am going to start reminding myself now that life is worth living. That my fun soul is going to remain at the top. I am going to work hard, and one day take over the gay bar once my dads retire and live an amazing life. That I will love again, and I have so much around me to appreciate.

I think going through such a scary trauma in life can actually change you for the better. You do not have to let your pain make you bitter. I swore that I would allow what happened to make me into the best version of myself. To spread light and joy to every human, because you never truly know what anyone is going through. To keep pushing in my own life to build a better future for myself. To see how precious life truly is and how each soul here really matters. To be there fully for those you love, especially other men. There is a reason why guys have a higher suicide rate. All those years of telling guys to just be tough is so damaging to their mental health. I now make an effort with my boyfriend, to always do my best to allow him to feel safe. To let him know that if he is ever struggling with pain, he can always let me know. That he does not have to be strong all the time, as no matter what gender we are, all humans have emotions. Feelings are not meant to be stuffed down. That it is okay to not be like Superman at every moment, and you can show your sadness and anger. All this made me realize, too, that you can never fully love another human without completely embracing their dark side. Our hard feelings can add an underlying strength to relationships. There is nothing more special than loving and embracing all parts of someone you love.

Chapter 19: Bryce

It was a last minute decision, but I feel it is needed. I am heading over to spend the weekend with mom. With everything that is going on lately, some family time seems to be a smart decision. I ran home for a few minutes after work to pack a bag before starting the three and a half hour trek to eastern Washington. The car ride is always so peaceful and this time the good vibes feel extra special. As I drive, I see the city lights fade behind me. The illuminating setting of Seattle disappears quickly, and before I know it, I am traveling in the remote wilderness. I passed thousands of evergreen trees and the wide open spaces of the Pacific Northwest. I open my window to let a breeze of the fresh air run across my face. I then sometimes realized nature is the best therapist there is. I decide to get some music going, and pull up the Spotify app on the car. I have a whole road trip playlist that is the perfect feel good one to play. It starts and the first song that pops on is "Life Is A Highway", the version from the movie "Cars." I smile as it starts because I am reminded of how much I loved that movie as a kid. I probably watched it at least 30 times. I am surprised that the DVD was not destroyed when I moved onto watching mainly superhero flicks. The joy it would give me though was impeccable. A perfect jam to start out with this trip home for the weekend.

I have about 20 more miles on the freeway and then the ride will almost be finished. The landscape started to transition to desert about thirty minutes ago, and I am reminded of how desolate this part of the state is. It is so big of a contrast between the many waterfalls and lakes that fill the western side to the barren land out here. The journey starts coming to an end as I enter the rural town that has been home to my mom for the past couple of years. I think mom told me the population is about 800, so as far as small towns in America go, this is one of the most quaint there is. Her town, Woodsville, fortunately, is very accepting. People out here do not differ too much from those in the city. There are even a couple of houses with gay pride flags on their lawn. I think to myself how beautiful it is to see the total acceptance. To realize that people can be free to love whoever they are attracted to and build a life that may be different from the majority but still just as beautiful. For true freedom to be embraced out here in a peaceful countryside town. That is what America is. As I pulled up into the driveway, I noticed mom standing on the porch. As soon as I get out of my car, I look up, and before I even grab my luggage from the back seat, mom begins to talk. "You finally made it, how was the ride, love?" "It was peaceful, and long." I then begin to walk up to the front door. "Come here dear" she says, before she wraps me into a brief but love filled hug. "I have some fresh pie on the counter for a snack if you would like some. It just came out of the oven less than an hour ago." After a stressful week, that sounds like an awesome idea. Mom always makes the best apple pie. She uses local apples and mixes a lot of brown sugar into it. It always comes out to be like a slice of heaven. The premade one I get from the bakery back at the market by me tastes like trash compared to the one I get when coming over here. Eating it adds such a special sense of comfort that can only come from the beauty of a loving home.

This time, as usual, it did not disappoint. The gooey apples and homemade pie crust filled my mouth up with so much deliciousness . There is nothing like some good old countryside desserts. After I finish up my slice, I head over to the den. Mom was watching the film Sleepless In Seattle. If I had ten dollars for every time I saw her watch that film, I would have a good paycheck by now. She says it is her comfort film and growing up and being in western Washington for many years makes the film more special to her. As with many women, romantic comedies are her favorite, but I think many more guys like them than we know. A lot of men are just scared to admit it, I believe, because of what society has ingrained into them. While I love big and exciting superhero movies, I am not afraid to admit I enjoy romantic comedies. They can be so cute and fun when done right. "What has been going on lately? How is life going?" as I was sitting on the couch. Before I give my answer, I think I should give the honest one or more of a white lie. I decided, because it is mom, it is better to go with the former, one of those options. "A lot has been happening lately." I know mom can sense the heaviness in my voice. Her face turns more sensitive, "Honey, what is going on? You know you can tell me anything." "Gosh, where do I begin? Well, first off, I have been offered a job promotion that would require me to move to Montana." "Well, that sounds exciting! Are you going to take it?" "See, that is why there is so much going on lately. On the surface, it sounds great, but several weeks ago I met this amazing lady. Her name is Carly, and there are so many sparks between us, but, of course, she has her life in Seattle, and now I do not know what to do."

A few moments of silence fell between us and I could sense mom carefully planning her response. I wonder how she will respond to this. Mom is loving and sweet but also has a brutal honesty she gives. "Oh honey, I had no idea you were seeing someone, first I need you to know

I'm so happy you found a wonderful lady. You are an amazing guy who only deserves the best. I know how much you have longed to find the right one."

Everything she already said is so true. I am a romantic. I have waited a while to find someone like this that I am truly compatible with. She then goes on to say some more. " I want you to know, though at the end of the day, whatever you choose to do is completely your decision, but you have to listen to your heart. Is a change of scenery and a better job position really worth it over than this wonderful thing you have happening now with Carly? Nobody can decide, expect you." Everything mom is saying now is so accurate. I pretty much knew all of it though, but hearing it from someone who truly loves you just hits different. I have all the answers I need. I guess all I can do now is listen to my heart. It is so torn on which way to go still and time is running out. Do I take a risk on love and building a life with Carly? "Thanks mom, I really needed to hear that. You are the best." "Of course sweetie, I really just want you to be happy and life can be so tricky sometimes in situations like these. Like life is not all sunshine and rainbows and I know you are stressed now, but in the end, I know you will do what is best for you. I am so proud of the man you have become, now let's finish enjoying the film." I smile at her before she presses play, and we enjoy the rest of Tom Hanks and Meg Ryan's iconic film.

The film finishes and by the time the end credits start rolling, I check my phone. It is already 11:30. I felt exhausted, and I walked over towards the patio and glanced out the window for a moment. I just wanted to soak in the peace of the area I am in. City life, even in one like Seattle, that is not as big as Los Angeles, can be crazy sometimes. It is such a different lifestyle than country living. I then look up at the sky and see so many stars illuminating the countryside. The star gazing out here is probably some of the best I have ever seen. It fills my eyes with a sense of joy I have not experienced in some time. I even caught the big dipper all lined up, creating a sense of superiority over me. I am reminded of just how small us humans really are compared to the grand scheme of the universe. I then looked over at mom and saw she had passed out in her recliner. I walked over there and threw the blanket that was lying on the couch. I turned off the kitchen light and patio one before heading upstairs to rest.

The next morning, I awoke to the aroma of pancakes as well as the countryside sun peeking through the blinds. The light begins to fill the house up in a beautiful way. It fills it up with a natural brightness that feels as good as a warm glass of lemonade on a hot summer day. I can smell that mom is cooking one of her amazing breakfasts. Hopefully it is the one I adore the most. Since I was young, I have been treated to her signature apple pancakes and smoked sausage. She knows it is one of my favorite things she cooks, so what a treat it would be if that is what I am smelling. I walked downstairs and saw mom over the grill, "Good morning sunshine, how did you sleep?" "Great, thanks for the lodging last night, it feels nice to be with some company this weekend." "You know you are welcome here anytime dear, that bed is always there for you." "How did I get so lucky to have a mom like you?" "I am finishing up your favorite apple pancakes, the smoked sausage is over there on the counter, if you want some as an appetizer you are more than welcome to, but the pancakes will be done in about five minutes." I decide to just wait to enjoy the full meal together, we then take our food out on the porch to enjoy a peaceful breakfast.

We then eat together and enjoy the fresh air. The smell of the wide open spaces out here just breathes a sense of liveliness to me, and we chow down on the yummy food. "So Bryce, are you planning to leave tonight or stay one more?" "I think I am going to stay one more night, probably leave in the morning around 10." "Sounds awesome, I was thinking tonight for dinner I will do some ribs and macaroni and cheese." "Sounds like heaven to me." I then walk in the house to put my breakfast plate in the sink. As I finish up doing that, I hear my phone ding, it is a text from Carly. "Hey Bryce, please call me whenever you get the chance."

Chapter 20: Cathy

Thursday afternoon 3:30 PM

Bryce is coming over tomorrow, which just had me thinking a lot about past events. I was really reminiscing about all the life we have lived. Also, how fast it has gone by keeps popping in my head too. Sometimes, even though I gave my world to him, as a parent, you still wish you could have protected them more. I truly never thought he would have had to face something so tragic, and at the worst age. You see Gerald passed at a time when he could still vividly recognize his dad and would have fond memories of him. I know how strong and how really special of a man my son is. I feel like it is typical for parents to say, my kid is so amazing, and we all have our own individualized unique gifts, but Bryce really is a different kind of man.

I flicked the light on and started walking down into the basement hoping I would find it, the special photo album. During the move, a lot of stuff got misplaced, and unfortunately, my oh-so-adored collection of pictures I had put together specifically with ones of Bryce and his father were one of the misplaced items. I rummage through the boxes that I had stored down here, a lot of them I have already searched through. I hope maybe I might have just missed it while searching, and it might appear in one of them. Still, nothing even close to that album is to be found.

As I head back over to the stairs, about to head back up, I pass by my old glass cabinet. I glanced over and happened to notice there were a couple of boxes on the bottom shelf. I opened up the door and reached down to the first one. Before I open it, I brush off a clump of dust. This one definitely does not look like it has been opened in quite some time. At the moment I rip off the tape and open up the top. I take out a couple of old TIME magazines I had saved from the early 2000s and then boom, it appears, the photo album I have been dying to find.

I make it up to my kitchen and begin to open up the album. As the pictures appear in my eyes, beauty fills my heart, like that feeling you get from hugging someone you love by the fireplace on a crisp fall day. I then make it to the page with pictures full of Bryce and Gerald on what would be the last family vacation for the five of us. It was one of the greatest trips we have done. I cannot help but smile so gleefully as the memories of it come flooding back into my mind. The trip was a mixture of both Florida and the Caribbean. We had both saved our vacation time for two years so we could make a big grand trip. I thought too, since the East Coast and Caribbean are not close, that it would be nice to see more than just Florida while we were already out there. We spent 5 days in Orlando before spending 5 more on Grand Cayman Island.

As I turn the pages I pass many heartwarming photos. From one of Bryce and Gerald sitting next to each other on the roller-coaster cart for Big Thunder Mountain to them building sand castles on the beautiful, tropical beach of Grand Cayman. I then am reminded of the joy Bryce always carried and also how he still holds a lot of that inner child beauty which is rare. See, no judgment, but there are a lot of people in this world that are like Grinches. Bryce was never that way though. Through everything, he still loves life. He has made a beautiful one for himself, bringing so much goodness to the world. Never once did I have the school call me about any bad behavior. Yes, he was and is a very emotional man, and sometimes I had to remind him that this emotional side is beautiful, but sometimes people are going to find it a lot to handle, his heart shines so much compassion.

As I continue to pass the pages and see pictures from Christmas mornings to birthday celebrations, I start to remember how sweet of a bond the two of them had. And how I know losing his father was such a heartbreaking moment for my son. I then remember the only time I had a real issue with him was after his dad passed. For about one year Bryce suffered from some pretty bad temper tantrums. It was a little scary at first because I had never seen him like that but in the end he did eventually overcome all his difficult feelings. I quickly realized at the time there was nothing wrong with him. Kids often process trauma in different ways from adults. When he was upset, and crying and yelling all I could do was comfort him, as any mother should do. Hold him and let him know his hurt is ok and his emotions are valid. Let him know how special he is and that he is going to be ok. During a couple of the outbursts he had, I did worry more though. One time he had a crying fit for almost an hour. The pain in his eyes was so hard to witness. You see, us parents are just human beings. We have feelings too and seeing such a young soul in so much distress can take a toll on your well being. I am grateful though that eventually his severe inner pain did start to subside. It was like one day the stormy cloud that was over him decided to move on, and the sun was slowly starting to try and make its way in.

Despite that year of struggles, the man he is today is amazing. I pray to God that the right women will come into his life and see his worth. I know how men can be and it might be hard for a lady to want a guy as sweet as him. Too, from my experience a lot of girls sometimes will like a bad boy. This is not always the case but I have had quite a few friends over the years who only want the super tough and assertive ones. Bryce is not that. Probably the complete polar opposite if I am being honest. It doesn't really matter though, his unique personality is what makes him such a beautiful soul. I know whatever woman chooses him will be such a lucky one but in the meantime the light he shines everywhere he goes and the value he brings to this world is oh so more than enough.

<u>Chapter 21: Carly</u>

In the emergency room, nurses walk by and computers beep constantly. The energy of the medical center adds a melancholic vibe that I absolutely despise. There is such a seriousness to being in a hospital and I absolutely hate it. The white walls and scrubs on the staff are soul crunching. The vital machines passing by and people all around you dealing with certain ailments is just depressing. How I wish I could be in the warm sun outside at the palm tree covered Laguna Beach right now instead of being trapped in this for-profit healthcare hell. Why are sick people all crammed into a building like this? Sometimes I think there is a more humane way to treat people that are dealing with health issues.

I do not know how the staff do this day in and day out. I do believe we all have our purpose in life though, and we need humans working here, but for me, I could never do it. It sucks because my Epilepsy has been doing great for about a year now. After my neurologist put me on the Haldol, I thought this was finally done. Boy, was I wrong. Today I had my longest one ever. It clocked in at a little over two minutes, which is not good. Worst of all, I had tripped over and hit my head on a table in my den, which led me to have a moderate concussion. This truly is not good. They had let me know that because I live alone, this could have ended a lot worse. Somehow I am doing quite ok and awake and breathing though. I believe wholeheartedly something bigger kept me safe and I am so grateful for whatever force that may have been.

The nurse told me about an hour ago that I would be staying here to heal for at least three days. Sometimes life can feel like it is all falling apart. Like you are dying with all this pain but not actually in the process of death. I have been blessed for most of my life. Yes, I had a medical condition, but most people have at least one. Nobody is invincible or has fully perfect health. With everything happening with Bryce though and now this, it feels like it is getting to be too much.

I hear my phone ring, and realize Bryce is actually calling. I jolted to it and picked up, "Hey Bryce" "Hey how are you?" "Not so well, I am sorry if I'm bothering you, but I really care about you despite what is going on and wanted to let you know I am in the hospital." A pause settles between us before he begins to speak "Good gosh, what happened? Are you going to be ok?" "I never told you this, but I suffer from epilepsy. I had my first seizure when I was just six and for years I went through different medications and treatments. A lot of them would work for a bit but then we would have to try another one. It is pretty severe, but my doctor finally put me on medication that was helping control them for like a year and a half. I never had gone that long without any so I thought this pill would be my saving grace. Well, today, I just had my worst one and hit my head too which led to a moderate concussion." Tears spill from my eyes as I tell all this to Bryce. It is hard because I know he is already dealing with a lot, but I have to let him know because I care about him. I did not even think about texting him earlier, I just did it because I know I love him. I always will whether he moves or stays. "I'm so sorry you are going through this now. I wish I could have been there with you. I'm actually here visiting my mom this weekend, but I can come visit you tomorrow if you like." I hear that he is about to break down in tears too. His voice is muffled, and I can sense all the pain he has now. "I would love to see you, and I hope you enjoy the rest of the time with your mom." "Thank you, Carly, and I am so sorry about everything I have put you through lately. I look forward to talking more in person." Without even thinking, I say "I love you." Through the tears he then replies "I love you too, my sweet Carly."

A couple of hours later, the doctor arrived in my room. Dr. Lee has been very thorough and compassionate since I got here. He did an initial examination earlier and now he has come back for an evening follow up. I hear a knock before he enters. "Good evening Carly, it is Dr. Lee, how are you holding up?" "Still a bit lightheaded but starting to feel better." "Well I'm not too surprised you took quite a fall and had a pretty major seizure earlier." He then goes on to check my reflexes, which all appear ok. "So you are healing pretty good, we are actually not going to admit you, but I want to keep you under observation in the Emergency room til at least Monday afternoon, we will then reassess and most likely discharge you then." I feel so relieved, it seems like I am getting better already which is such a blessing. "Alright I will see you tomorrow." "Have a good night doc." Well what a good follow up that was. I am glad my body is fighting through all the physical trauma well, because we only get them once. How grateful I am to be healing and how lucky I am to be safe right now.

I wake up the next morning with the nurse by my side and the blood pressure cuff doing the tight squeeze along my upper arm. "Sorry to wake you, just doing your morning vitals, get some more rest if you need it." My eyes gently open and close as I am fading in and out of a deep sleep. They then drift back into darkness and I fall back into a peaceful rest. A bit later, I woke up again, this time feeling way more rested. I gazed up at the clock and noticed it was around 11am. Then I look over towards the window and in the chair, to my surprise, Bryce is sitting right there. "Bryce, you made it." "I had to come Carly, how are you holding up?" "Pretty good actually the doctor gave an update yesterday and I should be discharged soon." He then gives a slight smile which seems to have a bit of relief in it, "Well I am so glad to hear that." He then moves his chair closer to me, and we sit there together. He puts his hand in mine and gives it a gentle squeeze before giving me a magical kiss on the forehead that feels as special as the vibes a romance movie will give you. "Everything's going to be ok, Carly."

My lunch then arrives on the tray. I am surprised to realize that the food at this hospital is pretty good. I mean I only went to one other hospital in California years ago when I had my first major seizure, but I remember the food being horrible there. If that is my fond memory of it, I assume that it really must have been pretty bad. I began to chow down on some of the chicken tenders that taste almost as good as ones you would get from a chain restaurant like T.G.I Fridays. "So how was the time with you mom?" I asked in between a bite. "It was actually excellent. I think with all that has been going on it really was needed and important for me to go." "That is good, sometimes family time with those who know us best can make all the difference." I then begin to finish up my lunch enjoying the side of macaroni and cheese that was given to go with the main course. Definitely better than the basic boxed kind. "So Bryce, have you decided? What day do they have to know by?" "Friday, so pretty much just about five days and no, by the looks of things, I probably won't know until Friday, when I am pretty much forced to." "Well, thank you for being honest with me, and thank you for being here with me today. You really do not know how much it means to me, my family cannot make it up to visit and Britney and Sara are away for a weekend girls trip." Bryce then wraps me in a hug. The feeling of love oozes over me in a way I have never experienced before. "Of course, Carly, and thank you for being you. You are the most special human I have known and every minute we share together feels like a slice of paradise."

Chapter 22: Bryce

I had to call out of work. Carly's discharge time was at 11am and I knew it would take longer than the one hour break I am allowed . I did not want her to take an Uber as I feel she really deserves to have someone she trusts bring her back home. As I pulled into the Green Fields Medical Center ER's main entrance, I saw her sitting on a bench with a folder in her hands, probably full of the discharge paperwork. I honked the horn once and waved over towards her. She then perks up and hops in. "Well, it feels good to be out of there, fresh air never felt better. I was so tired of breathing that recycled institutional oxygen." Hospitals can be a strange place and I cannot help to think that I understand her enthusiasm to be able to come home. When you think about it though, there is a strange beauty to medical facilities as well. I mean look at her coming out healed from a moment of destruction. New life starts in the hospital too, which is so beautiful, but they also showcase the hardest parts of humanity. Severe injuries from accidents and death are also a bold reality of so many events that happen there often. I guess every single thing in life has elements of light and darkness. Nothing is just either or.

As we pull up to Carly's apartment I feel a sense of wanting to stay there with her. She needs some comfort and to have someone to look out for her. This accident had me thinking, what if I was with Carly that day? What if I chose to spend time with her instead of going to my mom's house? I feel like God or the universe's plan was for me to have that time in the countryside, but why did the seizure have to happen during the one time I went away in months? Things sometimes do not have an explanation and trying to go down a rabbit hole to figure out what the greater meaning was, can be pointless. What has happened is finished. Now it is time to just live and let live.

"Are you doing anything now, because I was wondering if you wanted to spend some time together?" "Bryce, I am free, but I do not want us hanging out to add more stress to you now." "No, it is fine, I need to Carly, I just need to be here with you. We don't have to talk or do much if you prefer but please, I would love to come in ""Ok then if you think that it is going to be a good thing for you, let's just be together."

Once we get inside, we immediately head to the couch. The electricity is sparking again between us like the night we first made love. We then cuddle tightly, my arms are wrapped tightly beside her as we sit on the couch. "I am so glad you are ok." I whisper gently in her ear. "I am too, it was scary, but just glad it is over now." I then kiss her on the cheek. "What would you like for dinner?" "Let's just order some Sushi, Taki House on Doordash is the best." I ordered a few rolls and a can of orange soda for each of us.

About thirty minutes later, our dinner arrived. We then got to the table and enjoyed it together. After we finish up, we head to bed. We begin to cuddle again. The vibes are so comforting, and I know they are much needed by Carly after dealing with a lot of pain the past few days. Before I know it, she falls asleep with my arms wrapped around her. Even though she was healing in the hospital for a few days, I am sure the stress of all that happened to her was draining. I, on the other hand, cannot fall asleep that fast tonight. My mind begins to wander more about all that has happened over the past few weeks. From the job promotion offer to Carly's seizure and everything in between, it feels more like five years have passed.

I then got up and walked towards the den. The clock on the wall says 12:30 am. As I walked by, I noticed a bunch of papers on the table. I am usually not a nosy person, but I gaze over and see it is some of the discharge papers. I rumble through them a little because my curiosity is getting the best of me about what happened to her. I then got to a page with a written recommendation letter from Dr. Lee, her attending physician during her time there, it reads.

GREEN FIELDS MEDICAL CENTER
    7/27/2023
    CARLY O'CONNOR
    PATIENT ID # 59871270
    PHYSICIAN LETTER
    FOR PATIENT AND THEIR PROVIDERS RECORDS:

After treating the above-mentioned patient at our faculty for a severe epileptic seizure and moderate concussion, it is from my best understanding that from thorough medical evaluation that the previous condition the patient has may be worsened. This should be moderated with extreme caution. A follow up appointment with Neurology has been scheduled and should be kept and followed through with. In addition, I am recommending the patient should not be left alone, as she is at high risk for another seizure.With not having someone looking out for her, the risk of further injury is too major.

Sincerely,

Charles Lee MD- Green Fields Medical Center ER lead physician

I have to reread it again to make sure I got all that correctly. High risk for another one. Should not be left alone. Condition may have gotten worse. All of that is so serious. I hope to God this doctor is just being overcautious, but right now I see how badly she truly needs me. I am going to be there for her for as long as I can.

The next morning, I was sitting at the kitchen table. That was the scene for me all night as I was not able to sleep. If I had not read the letter I probably would have gotten at least a few hours of shut-eye, but by the time 4 am came, I knew it would not be worth it as I had to go back to work today.

A little while later, I hear the door of Carly's bedroom creak open, "Bryce? What are you doing out here sitting at like 4:30?" Her voice is mellow. I notice a sense of disorientation in her. I can tell she was still half asleep. "I could not sleep, too much on my mind." I then noticed her glance over to her hospital discharge papers. It would be hard not to notice how messy they looked compared to the neat pile they were in before I rumbled through them." Did you look through my discharge papers?" Her intuition is sharp, like a lot of women. "I am sorry, but yes, I did, I did not expect it to be anything major, but Dr. Lee is worried about your condition, like more than I thought." I know he is, but I think he may be exaggerating. We should wait to see what Dr. Robinson says at the follow-up tomorrow." "You had an over two-minute seizure. I did some research into epilepsy. That is bad. And if I do decide that the move is the route I will take for my life, who is going to watch you?" In an instance, she begins to look more alert. It is like this conversation is her alarm clock, but I know this is not a pleasant way to awaken. "That is not for you to worry about , Bryce! Look, you have to do what is best for you. I know you know this for sure at this point and, just so you are aware, Britney said she would be fine with living here a few days a week to look out for if that is really what is needed. The other days that I will need supervision, I could reside with Sara." "You think all that pressure is fair for your friends?" "Again, Bryce, that is my concern. They have been my best friends for years. We have a special bond that you probably would not be able to understand."

I then felt a tinge of sadness run through me. "So that is what you think of me then? That I cannot understand, which basically means you think I do not have a good heart?" "That is not what I said, Bryce. I fully understand what you are going through! How being an adult is so damn hard at times and a better job is important. There is a lot of confusion too, because we have only known each other for like a month and a half. However, I do not think you understand how rare a connection like this is. And how I feel confused right now too." I then feel a sense of despair. "It is so hard being an adult, and I'm sorry for adding any additional pain to your life. She then walks closer to me and wraps me in a hug. "You are not doing anything wrong, I just don't need you to worry so much, I know that is what you do because you are a good man, but please do not let my life and the struggles I have prevented you from living your one life to the fullest." We then stand there, in silence, just wrapped in each other's arms for two minutes. I can hear nothing else but the birds chirping outside as a sense of epic comfort covers us. Those two minutes felt like so much longer and in that hug, we both realized just how strong love can be in times of struggle.

I walk into work, despite really hating the fact I have to be here today. The office walls end up feeling confining, almost like being in a tight jail cell. My mind feels the same way with thoughts of the choice I have to make as well as the reality of Carly's medical condition suffocating me. Once I start working, though, the distraction it brings from everything else going on feels a bit good. I headed over to the break room for a quick mid-morning glass of water. As I am about to throw away my cup, I bump into Crystal. "Good morning" she says in her normally upbeat voice. "Hey." I then notice her face change as I know she can sense something is not right with me, her best friend. "My friend, tell me what is up? This does not seem like you." "Just the drama with Carly, there is just so much going on lately. I don't want to give away too much of her business, but she has been dealing with stuff and on top of that you know I have a ton of anxiety now." Crystal let's put a gentle sigh. "So you really like this girl a lot, don't ya? See when you told me about everything and the promotion offer, I was enthusiastic because I wanted you to live fully. I thought maybe that is what you needed, which is why I may have come across as inconsiderate." "Yeah you kind of did." "But the other reason why is that I was not sure this girl you just met was worth sacrificing your life for. You care so deeply, Bryce. More than most guys I have ever met. You are sensitive, but fun and adventurous. You have taught me to love the Pacific Northwest, a region you truly appreciate in a way that if I moved out here and did not meet you, I do not think I would have. You are an empathic soul, and now I see how much this woman means to you." "Thank you for saying all that, Crystal. It really means a lot" "In the end, I know you will make the right decision. Maybe you guys will find a way to make it work, despite the distance, but it is your destiny that is being written now. Just know I will always love you, my amazing friend." My eyes begin to tear up as she reaches out to hug me. "Love you too."

Chapter 23: Carly

I was advised by Dr. Lee, it would be best not to head back to work until Thursday. He informed me that given the severity of the seizure mixed with the moderate concussion, some additional rest for a few days would be important. I decided to sit on my porch and read some of a book I started by Nicholas Sparks. Sometimes a good romance novel can really make you feel better, especially in times of hardship. The pure loving vibes that come from the words written on the pages end up filling me up with some much needed love. I look out over my balcony to the sea of evergreen trees and just soak in the view and pine-scented air for a moment. Despite all that is happening around me and whatever the future holds, this moment is special. There is a lot to be grateful for even while here on deck in my one-bedroom apartment. Just taking in this brings such beauty to my soul.

I wonder how Bryce is doing. After our little talk this morning, he seemed upset. I hope the office is not too chaotic today, because, lately, I know he already has so much on his plate. I really hope the days at Seaside Programming are not filled with any additional drama. Stress is not good for our bodies and working a full-time office job already brings more than enough of that than we need. My phone began to ring. Immediately, I think it is probably Bryce, but to my surprise, it is actually my mom. "Sweetie, how are you holding up." She says in her nurturing voice. As I get older, I see where my caring ways come from.

Although, I have not really had a chance yet to show a romantic partner my heart, I know deep down it is there. Not having a serious boyfriend by now though sometimes makes me question if I am loving enough though. Like am I just too focused on having fun and enjoying life and I really am not that

sweet? I think having doubts is normal though. We all have our own insecurities.

My mom is a good one. I really got lucky because not everyone gets such an amazing mother fighter. I know, I have learned so much from having her as my parental figure. I had a friend, Ally, in college for a couple of years whose mom traumatized her. From bullying and being a mean girl to her and even her brother, I know how hard some people have it with their families. It is important to remind myself just how fortunate I am. I really have had a pretty easy life. If I am being honest, the hardest thing I went through was when we lost our family dog, Ziggy, six years ago. There are so many worse things people go through. Yes, having epilepsy is also hard to deal with, but in all honesty most people have some sort of health conditions. It could always be worse too, as there are people who struggle with other scary disorders like Multiple Sclerosis.

From extreme poverty to physical abuse, I really am a fortunate person to have not dealt with any of that. In hard moments like what happened a few days ago, I am reminded of how special it is to have people that care so much. Whether it happens to be biological or chosen, we all need at least one compassionate human that we can lean on when things get rough. I have such a good family and that is a lot more than most people have.

"I am doing fine, will be back to work on Thursday and I do not feel all too bad. I still feel a bit lightheaded though from it all, but that is going away." " I am so glad to hear that dear, on Friday evening me and your dad were wondering if it would be ok if we came up and spent the weekend with you. We found a really cheap flight from Spirit and can book it today."

I remember Friday is the day. The day when the decision should be made by Bryce. At this point, I really started to let go. To realize that is for him and only himself to decide. So having the parents visiting, up here, despite what is going to happen with everything else, would be a beautiful thing. "I would love it if you guys came, but are you sure you have the availability? Just want to make sure.." "Yes darling, we had nothing planned for this weekend so it would be an honor to spend it with our sweet lady. We are going to book it, and we will see you probably around 9pm Friday evening." "Alright, thanks so much! I cannot wait to hug you guys!" I then hung up the phone feeling excited to know that I would have them to be with soon. I have not told them about Bryce yet, so they do not know if he chooses to move, having this time together will be all the more special. You have got to treasure those around you because you never know when it will be the last time they are out of your life.

I headed over to my dreaded appointment with Dr. Robinson. It is frowned upon for a couple of reasons. One, I am so ready to just move on with my life. This is not fully living a good life, dealing with medical institutions so much. I know health challenges are part of most people's lives to a certain degree, but I have been tired of dealing with one since I was a kid. I am ready to get back to working hard and playing even harder. It also has me nervous because I really am hoping my epilepsy will not get worse. Part of me really hopes Dr. Lee was totally wrong and that this was just a one-time setback. "Ms. O'Connor?" the medical assistant said into the waiting room. I stood up, and we headed into one of the examination rooms. "I'm Cynthia, I work with Dr. Robinson, so you are here to follow up after a seizure and concussion, lead you to the emergency room. Is that correct?" "Yes, that is" I replied. "Alright, let me just check your blood pressure and temperature and then the doctor will be right in." She then does a quick vital check which all appear to be completely ok.

A few minutes later, I hear a knock on the door, "Hey Carly, how have you been?" he says in his upbeat voice. I have only been here three times, but this man seems so cheerful, either he really loves his paycheck, his job or is just a bubbly guy by nature. "I mean doing great, starting to feel a lot better from the incident." "Great, that is wonderful to hear, so let us get right to business, " Dr. Lee sent over all the papers from the emergency room. He is worried your epilepsy is getting worse. We are going to do another EEG to see if there's been any change, but I do not think that is the case. I am thinking we may just need to increase the haldol to a higher dosage. Let me do a quick examination though." I feel a huge breath of relief wash over me like a warm gentle wave in The Bahamas brushing into me on a sunny day. He does his thing, feeling parts of my body and using that hammer thing to check my reflexes. He then lets me know that everything looks fine on my body right now from this examination. I leave the office feeling grateful as the sun shines down on me. All of a sudden, it feels like my life is just getting started again. Like all the darkness from the past few days, it is being lifted away, and I am ready for life again despite what bumps may come my way in the future.

Later that evening, Britney and I decided to go to the mall for some retail therapy. It seemed like a nice celebratory thing given the good neurology follow-up and just to get out of the house after all the health drama. I also thought it would be helpful to chat with her about life. She is the more honest best friend. Just getting some advice from her can really make a big difference. Sometimes you need that person who will keep it real with you and not sugar coat life, especially in difficult moments. As I pulled up to the mall, I noticed Britney standing outside the main entrance. We walked in and decided to get some dinner first at the food court. I run to the sushi place while she gets some Chick-fil-a. I then order my food and, after I pay, and get it. I glanced over to the Chick-fil-a stand and noticed she was not there anymore. I looked around to see if I could find her. I then notice that she is waving over at me, "Carly, over here!" I rush towards her and take a seat. Despite having so much on my mind, I am pretty good at hiding it. I guess I'm good at having some emotional control, I would like to think. We then began to enjoy our different lunches. "I'm so glad you are ok, I heard from Sara you took quite a hit with the seizure and concussion." "Yeah it was a lot, but thankfully feeling so much better, the rest has really helped all the injury symptoms subside." "Well, just be careful, that all is no joke, I mean a seizure and concussion is a lot of stuff happening to your head. I want you to keep taking it easy." Sometimes Britney is so honest, which can be a lot, but I know she means well. "I got you, don't you worry, I'm going to be ok."

We then begin to finish up our food, "There is something I really could use your advice on though, the Bryce ordeal. We both look at each for a moment. I can tell she is ready to pour so much truth out, like Britney does best. "So you are still stuck on him, I totally get it, there is a special connection, and I am so happy you got to experience that." "I am too." I reply "But we are not in high school and what he is being offered can change his life in a way that you might not be able to." I don't really know how to take that and feel a little annoyed by her response "What the heck is that supposed to mean?" "What I mean is a job promotion to a better and raise like that is a beautiful thing that can enhance his life, you are an amazing person, I know you I know that, and I even think you completely know how special you are. Sometimes, though there is more to life than just love, but then on the flip side, there is more than just work too. If he does choose to move, you can either take this situation and look at it as something heartbreaking or something beautiful. You got to experience this special, romance movie like instant bond that not everyone gets. Life could end for us all tomorrow Carly, like the sun could explode, and the earth be disappeared for good, but for nearly two months you had this strong bond." I then nod and am briefly left speechless. We did have so many beautiful moments together and, even though our time may have been brief, maybe there is a reason for this time we were placed in each other's lives. Like I know I am just me, and he is who he is and if I really care about him, letting him do what is best for his life is the most loving thing I could ever do. "I mean that is the most honest and healthy way to look at the situation." I replied. I then realized if it was not for Britney I do not think I would have ever looked at the situation from such a beautiful viewpoint. Love from friends can be just as powerful as that from a romantic partner and I think right now I am just fully able to comprehend that. Love.

We then throw away our trash and head down to Forever 21. For a weekday evening, the mall was pretty busy. "I guess Amazon really is not destroying traditional shopping the way people think", I say playfully. "I guess not, which is pretty dang shocking because I would take the two day prime shipping for something, over coming out here any day of the week." I then burst out into a laugh "Come on, there is more fun to life when you come out and enjoy a shopping outing than just wait for a package to be delivered by some giant corporation." "If you say so my friend, if you say!"

We made it down to Forever 21, the store at this mall is probably the biggest one of there's I have seen. It has two big levels and enough clothes in there to keep you looking through them for years. Not too long after we walked in, I spotted a cute tank top with a fancy Santa Monica pier art design on it. "Oh my god, isn't this the cutest?" "It's nice, but it will fit your style better than it would me. I like the design though." Britney is more into darker colors, she is not goth but just prefers simpler outfits. You could say our styles are a bit opposite. I operate on more colors as well as shirts with more elaborate designs, while you will see here in more striped dresses and maybe some polka dots. Britney decides not to splurge today. "You sure you do not want anything?' " Yeah, I just got a JC Penny clothing haul delivery, so I will probably be good probably til the fall. "Hey, do you want to see what is playing at the movie theater?" I ask her as I am handing the cashier my debit card. "Sure, maybe we can catch something good if our timing is right." "Awesome, we won't know til we go up there."

"Do theaters play anything else except action and horror movies these days?!" Britney says. "I mean I kind of have to agree with you, they are forgetting about us comedy and romance fans!" That is one thing we for sure have in common, our movie taste is almost identical." "I mean that new animated movie, Sammy Shark's: Crazy Adventure starts in 20 minutes, it does look cute and funny." "I guess we will settle for the sweet family film." I say with a big smile. We then ordered some popcorn and soda and headed over to our theater.

"I thought it was fun, it definitely was made for adults too and was not completely for kids. "I agree, it is always nice when the film crew thinks about the other people that will enjoy it other than the under-six-year-old crowd." We then exit the mall, with the Mountain View Shopping Center sign lit up brightly beside us underneath the star filled night sky. I reached out and gave her a big hug before we parted ways for the evening. "Thank you for today, it was so fun!" Britney looked a bit shocked. I only rarely hug her like this, so I can understand why she may be confused. "Of course, I hope you continue to feel better, oh and try not to worry too much about Bryce. I know your life is going to be special and amazing, no matter what happens! You got this!" "That means so much, text me when you get home safely." I then blew her a kiss as we headed towards our cars and I heard her yell, "I love you!"

<u>Chapter 24: Britney</u>

I arrived in Seattle when I was just 19. The west coast was calling me and I had to get as far away from Sheffield as possible. Growing up in the countryside of western Pennsylvania was not what one may have initially expected. People have in mind this idea of rural life being some peaceful world where everything is perfect. You are surrounded by nature, there is no city rush, it all should be a great way to live, right? Well, in my case, growing up was more of an actual farmland hell than heaven. My mom and dad fought constantly. It was so traumatic for me as a kid for that to be my first insight into a relationship. There was no love involved and I have no idea why two people who have so much dislike towards one another end up staying together. Toxic would be an understatement. Slamming doors, cursing and yelling were all something that became part of my life. That was completely horrible because no kid deserves to be around such scary behavior from two adults for their whole childhood.

The funny thing too about it all was neither of my parents were alcoholics. As I get older it has become clearer to me that dysfunction does not just come from abusing a substance. No. People can create chaos from other means too. In their case, they just were not compatible. So them not being happy with the life they created ended up making it horrible for their own kids they chose to have. They met in seventh grade during a youth group at their conservative church in town. I have heard from people that by the time they both were in tenth grade they did not even seem that into each other. When they were younger, though, the youth group leader would go on and on about how important it is to find someone who also loves Jesus, so, in a way, they kind of felt forced to stay together. I have nothing against believing in a God or choosing to attend religious gatherings, there can be some good that comes from. However, there is no denying that religion has also caused so much unnecessary destruction for parts of humanity.

"Why do the meals you cook always taste like crap?" "Why can't we go on more dates?!" "Why don't you cuddle with me more?!" Those are just a couple of the things my parents would yell at one another during their weekly screaming matches. I would always have to be the one as well, to protect my younger sister, Ally, from it all. I would shield her ears and take her up to my room, and then sometimes the police would come. Our neighbors were not too far away and people wanted their peace in the countryside. I would not blame them though. They had even been kind enough to call and make sure everything was ok. Once mom said it was all good, they would ask politely if they could please stop the screaming. Well, those two rude adults could not, so they had it coming.

The worst of it all too would be the few times they got arrested for disorderly conduct. You cannot cause such destruction in the world and get away with it. During my teen years, I would try to tell my mom how upset everything was making me and how badly I just wanted them to get along, and her response would pretty much always be "life is not a fairytale sweetheart, get over your feelings." I would think to myself then, why do some people have kids if they treat them in such a horrible manner.

Before I had graduated from high school, I knew I wanted to go away from college. Pittsburgh was not too far, but it felt far enough from the destructive small town life I was living. I applied for any scholarship I could and, by the grace of God, I was able to ensure that about seventy percent of my tuition to the University of Pittsburgh would be covered.

One day in December of my freshman year, I will never forget what happened. So I was lying on my bed reading a book and out of nowhere, bang, my door slams open. I looked up and it was my mom! She starts yelling about how I have not called her in months and how she is so over being my mom. I could not believe how any person, even a family member could have the nerve to barge in and be so disrespectful. Mind you, my roommate was sitting right there. I then yelled at her to get the hell out of here before I contacted the campus police and at that moment she knew she had better leave. I knew she could sense the seriousness in my tone and how I was not afraid to call. In that instance, I also knew it was time for me to leave Pennsylvania for good.

I had to transfer schools. It was a big decision to make, and one that was a little scary too, but ultimately more liberation filled me than fear when I decided to go through with it. The only thing that was going to really suck about this was telling my girlfriend Cassandra. She was here at the University of Pittsburgh too, and I know she always wanted to stay in Pennsylvania. One time, when we were at the county fair together in Junior year of high school, we sat on top of the ferris wheel, and she just started telling me about her future. She went on about how she loves it out here and how she wants to get a nice house a little bit outside Pittsburgh in the countryside. We took in that view together as the nice summer breeze came across and at that moment, it felt like we were on top of the world. I felt the beauty of it all too, but now looking back, part of me wanted to say this is not where I want to build my life. That I want to get the hell out of here and go to another state and forget about anything to do with Pennsylvania.

When thinking about states where I would want to move to Washington came to mind. For one, the West Coast is probably as far as you can get from Pennsylvania while still staying on the mainland USA. Two, I do love the natural beauty of my home state, so I wanted to go somewhere scenic. To be honest, the beauty of Washington is incomparable to Pennsylvania. Yes, I guess every state does have its own special natural features. I mean there is a song called America The Beautiful, but the scenery is unique up here. From rainforests, to such a rugged coastline and towering mountains, when I moved here the beauty added a peace I think I really needed after living in survival mode for so long.

I will never forget the day though I told Cassandra about the move. I had called her to come to my dorm room and I do not think she had any idea of the news that was about to come. She cried and yelled, going on about the beautiful life we were supposed to build out there and how I do not need to leave when our relationship brings so much beauty right here, and it felt like she did not see how important it was for me to get out of there. I understand too why it would be hard for her. Cassandra did not come from a broken family. Her parents owned a sit-down burger and steak restaurant a couple towns over that has been passed down for generations. Her parents really celebrated the business and gave Ally so much purpose. So it may be hard for someone like that to grasp wanting to move away to the different lifestyle of the West Coast.

I decided to switch to the University of Washington that February. I got a U-Haul and just drove out there. It was about a 40-hour total trip and the journey across America was stunning. The furthest I ever traveled was to Maine once when I was a kid. That and besides two trips to Ocean City, New Jersey were actually the only times I left Pennsylvania. Driving past the wide open spaces of the Western part of the country was so surreal. It added some moments of beauty I had never experienced after going through such a traumatic childhood. I suffer from episodes of depression too, from everything, but I will never forget the amazement that I was filled with during that trip. For a couple of days it felt like all my depression was wiped away. I knew that once I got to Seattle life would not all be sunshine and rainbows, but after such a crazy first 19 years, I felt like great freedom was about to come amidst all the pain I had overcome. I had a sense that Cassandra was going to be just ok too. While I really did love her and will always be there if she needs me as a friend, I feel that the breakup I caused would be great for her in the long run too. She is a special woman, and I know she will find someone back there to build a special life with her. I think though that having a taste of freedom for her to really have a moment to find herself could be very healthy. At the end of the day we come into this world alone and out, and while romance is beautiful, so is knowing and embracing your full self.

Getting adjusted to Washington did take some time for me. Although a lot of them were amazing changes to embrace One, the culture out here is so different. Every single church I have seen in my six years out here is an LGBTQ pride flag. In western Pennsylvania near Sheffield, I think I have seen one, maybe two out of the 70 of them I have passed. There is such an emphasis on being connected to nature in the Seattle area too. That adds to a special relaxed lifestyle. Yeah, my home state is pretty nature centered too, but it is just a different vibe over here. I mean the two areas around 3,000 miles a part so there are bound to be some differences. There is also a sense of not focusing so much on societal constructs which has been so beneficial to my healing process.

What helped me so much out here was the change of meeting such an amazing friend as Carly. I will never forget meeting her. I was out at a rock concert downtown, and she was dancing the night away with Sara. I just sensed such a fun energy going on that kept making me smile big, like when you are watching your favorite comedy movie, just this fun energy. I just went over and said hello and that I love your dance moves and from then the three of us have been inseparable. I became like their third musketeer and added a different energy that they really benefited from. We all just appreciated it and meeting that night was such a moment of fate. It can be hard to make friends as an adult, life is just different, and we are all hardwired from our upbringings, but sometimes people are just meant to be best friends, and I am so glad we crossed paths, even though I truly thought it was already predestined and just meant to be.

Chapter 25: Bryce

After work, I decided to do something to help with the stress going on lately and head to Discovery Park. I really was reminded how beautiful this stretch of land is during the time we spent there. As I park my car near the lighthouse, the backdrop looks amazing with the sun beginning to set behind the forest. I get out and walk along the stretch of beach towards the bluffs and look out over the water way. The peace of nature fills my soul like a crying child comforted by their mother. I then lay my backpack on the sand and open it up to take out a beach blanket. I unfold and then sit on it as the sky begins to dim and the day begins its descent from brightness to dark.

Just sitting there on the beach proved to be utterly relaxing. There were not many people there so that was nice as it really allowed me to clear my mind. I then think back to the day when I first came here in middle school. The feeling of me and my buddies running along the beach throwing the football to one another comes to me in an all consuming way. It was with Chase and Brian that day, I wondered for a second how they are holding up in adulthood too. With all the responsibilities now and challenges from moving on from youth, I hope they are doing well. I have not talked to them in quite some time but I happen to stumble upon a post from Chase on Facebook every so often. I remember seeing some pictures once in a while from an ATV riding trip or him sharing videos from a rock concert so I guess he is probably doing fine.

I then remember the joy that filled all three of us that day. How we did not have a care in the world. How it was the first time we hung out alone and our parents were all having to let go of us as we were beginning to become our own individuals. Then the memory of us running through the woods starts coming. With the dense greenery around us and we all feeling that crazy excitement. Gosh, I just want to hold on to that feeling. Because lately life's more challenging elements have been getting in the way, but I know I can access that joy anytime. The pain of the world cannot overtake that inner beauty we are all born with.

The sun is about to be fully away for the night, so I begin to fold up my blanket and walk back over to the parking lot. I pull out of the park feeling a renewed sense of myself. It is time to take back my joy. To know that I am not going to let darkness take over who I am. In a way going through all of this now, is giving me a sense of strength I never knew I had. These past several weeks really have been filled with my first true rough patch as an adult. With that though has been some of the most amazing beauty, having Carly with me and isn't it true that the most beautiful things in life are interwoven with some of the most all consuming pain? I mean look at the man I have become without my dad. Like my mom had said she is so proud of me and I am proud of myself too. There is so much more to life than just heartbreak. I think now I am truly seeing that in the most powerful way possible.

I made it home and feel so ready now. Ready to embrace what I choose to do with my life from now on. Ready to know my heart always makes the right decision. When I listen to the light, it always guides me to where I am supposed to be in the world and the stars for my destiny will truly shine through, and that I am capable of whatever changes come my way.

After work on Friday, I decided to head over to the waterfront near the sculpture park. This is a nice thing to do to help get my focus off the offer decision and more onto the joy of life. As I walk around, I once again am amazed at all the eccentric and interesting designs that these artists came up with. It really showcases just how creative humans can actually be. I then found a bench to sit down on to look out over the waterway. The sun was shining bright in the background, filling the city with a colorful joy which far differs from the rainy season this region is given for a full six months. I then get up and walk back towards the sculptures and where more of the city skyscrapers are. Although it feels different coming here alone I think I now notice solo dates can be so refreshing. Just getting to have some time to yourself doing a fun activity can feel so liberating. You do not always need someone by your side to enjoy the fun things in life.

I started to get hungry as I was ready to grab some food. Up the hill there is this great coffee shop that also has some fresh sandwiches and I really felt in the mood for one of them and a delicious iced latte. As I was about to head over there something stopped me in my tracks though. I was in disbelief to see who it was but there she appeared, Carly O'connor, looking like she was about to head down to the waterfront too. It has been a couple days since we last talked and once again, she is brought into my life, face to face with no way of not sending a text now.

Chapter 26: Carly

"Bryce? Is that you ? What are the odds?" I walk towards him and the two of us stand face to face. The waterfront surrounds us while an odd feeling of distance is felt which seems a bit strange. I get the sense that he may be speechless from either one of two things. It could be us meeting like this, so randomly in the middle of the city, or from some other hardship in his mind. A moment of silence then falls between us. "So what are you doing over here?" He asked me with his voice having more of a lowness with it. I can sense there is a bit of awkwardness for him, and I totally understand. To me it feels like another sign we are meant to be together, to him it probably adds some more confusion because I realized today has been the day he will either deny or accept the transfer.

"I was just actually coming over here to pick up some dinner, it was my first day back to the office and it was beautiful outside so I just thought it would be nice to walk over to get it before heading home." "It really is a nice evening out, like the literal perfect weather." "Thank God it's Friday!" I say trying to shift the energy to become more positive. "Yes, Friday is here thankfully." he replies. "Carly, are you doing anything tomorrow?" "By the looks of my schedule this weekend, I only have plans for Sunday. Britney, Sara and I are going to check out that new retro arcade by Taki House." "Ok then, be ready tomorrow for me to pick you up at your place at 7:30." I then feel surprised, I have never seen Bryce be this mysterious. "Wait, what for?" "Just be ready then, trust me you won't be disappointed." He then hugs me goodbye, "I hope you will be ready then, I will be waiting by your apartment!" He then begins to walk away. "Okay! I guess I will see you then mystery man, I am very intrigued now to see what you have up your sleeve!" He smiles brightly "I will see you soon!"

I then started to head home and throughout the drive my mind cannot stop thinking about what we will be doing tomorrow so early on a Saturday morning. Maybe he has some good news to share about him not taking the transfer? Maybe he is trying to spend some more time together before he moves to Montana? Who knows? Maybe it is best to just put all that aside and just embrace whatever it is he is coming over to do. He did seem more cheerful than I had seen him in a while, so that makes me even more curious to see what will happen.

I got home and decided to watch something on Netflix for a distraction. I noticed I had not watched The Kissing Booth 3 and thought it would be fun to watch. The first two were so much fun and filled with a lot of infectious joy. I feel like the third one will be just as sweet as it really is such a beloved franchise. The films really provide such a joyful escape and movies like that are so special. I honestly cannot see how anyone can enjoy watching a man named Jason running through the woods slashing people for ninety minutes. To each their own I guess, but I prefer happy films. I am not a horror fan in the slightest.

A little over halfway in, though, I felt my eyes beginning to shut. I realize I am already passing out. I fought for a few moments to try to stay awake because I truly love the movie so far, but it's not working out. I gently click the pause button before slowly drifting off. After such an eventful week, I am sure my body can still use some extra rest.

I woke up to a slight buzzing sound. I then hear it again, and it begins to fully awake me to full consciousness out of my deep sleep. I checked my phone and looked to see it was 7:40. Oh crap, I think I am late. I then ran down the stairs to open the door and noticed Bryce standing there. He has on some hiking boots and a Green Day t-shirt and some light blue shorts as well. Even at early in the morning, he looks so effortlessly handsome, but I am also wondering why the hiking boots? I have never seen them with those on, even on our first date to Discovery Park, where they could have been necessary. "Hey, so sorry for the delay, I say I can be ready in like 20 minutes." "That is fine he, I will be waiting down here ready to go whenever you are."

I then ran upstairs and tried to get ready as fast as ever. I opted out to skip make-up today, thinking it is not that important. I put on a pink tank top as well as some jogger sweats. For some reason, something in my gut is telling me it is a good idea to wear something comfortable for whatever he has in store for us today. I brushed my teeth and grabbed an envelope with something special in it, I was hoping to give him. I head back down and quickly hop into the front seat of his car. "Well, that was quick, I do not know if I ever saw a lady get ready that quick." "Well, I guess now you have." I reply in a fun teasing manner. "Did you have any breakfast?" "You really think I could get ready that fast and eat something?" "Alright that is true, where do you want to stop, we can stop anyplace you want?" "It would help me to know where we are going, so I don't make you go out of the way too much." He then smiles brightly at me and says "Do not worry about that, this is your day, just tell me what do you want for breakfast?"

I decided we should head for some place more basic that I actually enjoy and have us stop at an Ihop. We pull up and head right in. "Table for two please" he says, and then we walk over to our booth. "Bryce, what is going on? I am so confused about what is happening ""Just enjoy yourself, we are going on a little special journey today." "Can I at least know where?" "Somewhere you will love, and you are going to find out what that is soon enough." His sense of playfulness puts me at ease and also fills me with an excitement as to where we will be going. Our food comes out pretty quickly. As with a lot of chain restaurants, when the food arrives I think to myself, how did they cook it so fast?

I opted for the country fried steak and eggs while Bryce got the bacon temptation omelet. We finish up pretty quick and I notice he must have not had any breakfast either. "Ready to rumble now?" "You know it" I reply, and before I know it we are back on the freeway heading to the mystery place.

I noticed we had been heading north, which first got me thinking, are we heading to Canada? I mean that could be a fun day trip and would be quite the adventure so that definitely could be an option. "Any song requests?" "Can you play my favorite Britney song, Till The World Ends please?" The beat begins to start, and the party banger begins to blast from the speakers as we travel along the interstate. "That is such a bop, I am going to sound old by saying this, but it is actually true that pop music used to be better, they do not make songs like that anymore." "That is true, but art always evolves I guess." "Right but why now is so much of the music is dark and depressing, maybe that is why people are more miserable these days." "Well I guess people are enjoying that kind of stuff, maybe Gen Z is to blame." I then giggle and think I hope one day those big dance bangers will come back to the mainstream more.

As the drive continues, my curiosity deepens more, to almost a state of childlike wonder. "Can you please already let me know where you are taking me? We have been driving for so long already." "We are almost there, trust me, you won't be disappointed." I looked out the window and started to notice signs for North Cascades National Park. I then realized I thought I had figured out the special place he was taking me

My assumption proves to be right. We begin to fully enter the park. The mountains and forest begin to fully surround us, as the unspoiled natural beauty becomes unbearingly stunning. Signs for trailheads and recreation areas start to become normal as we drive deeper into the wilderness. "So a national park trip is what you had up your sleeve today." I playfully say. He then continues to drive, "I think you are going to like what else I have up my sleeve today for us here."

The towering snow-capped peaks continue to appear, one after another, making the landscape seem like a slice of heaven right here in America. Bryce then turns off the main drag, heading down a side road. We then pulled into a parking area. "I want to take you on one of my favorite hikes ever, if that is okay?" I felt a tinge of excitement fill up. The last time I went to this park, I must have been 12. We did not explore too much of it since we were on vacation, and we only set up a day to see it. Given the size of most national parks in America, it probably could take a lifetime to see it all. So to say I am ecstatic to be back is an understatement. As an outdoors-loving girl, who dreams of seeing all of America's most beautiful sites, it feels great to be back to see more of this one.

"So which trail is this called?" I asked. "We are doing one of the most iconic and stunning ones, I believe in probably all the world, The Cascade Pass." I feel a burst of joy. So many travel influencers I follow have talked about and shown footage of this one. I am sure Bryce did not know this, and it may be another coincidence of our strong, spiritual connection, but this is hands down a bucket list place for me to have been dying to visit. I remember even watching a full length YouTube video showcasing the awesomeness of this one. It feels utterly surreal now to actually be here now about to do it. I cannot wait to be standing there with him, being consumed by the towering peaks everywhere around us.

"No way! Bryce, you have no idea how long I have wanted to do this trail!" I exclaimed, my voice close to a scream. Then, without any hesitation, I ran towards the trail entrance. "Come on, let's go! We have got no time to waste", I then really yelled back at him. He slowly stomps over to me with a smile on his face. I feel like I probably looked like a kid on Christmas morning leaping out of bed down to all the new toys. At that moment, I fully realized how special the most simple things in life can actually be. Here in the fully naturally landscaped park, the sense of joy overflows me to a point where I feel fully alive.

Chapter 27: Together

The trail takes us deep into the forests and mountains, painting a scene of utter tranquility that only a park this majestic could. A field of wildflowers comes up on the left side, down in a valley which makes you feel like you have been transported to another planet. The medley of yellow and pink petals within a giant field creates a sense of beauty that looks like a scene from a painting you would see on a museum wall. We are at the two-mile mark now, which means we have about a mile and a half to go. "This trail is like three and a half miles each way for a total of seven", Bryce lets Carly know. They continue to pass more valleys as the trek continues. "Want some trail mix?" he asks. "Sure, I would love that." I then begin to munch down on it, which actually gives a little burst of energy. Definitely helpful on a long, adventurous hike.

As the two of them near the main overlook, they end up passing a herd of Elk. The family looks to be without a care in the world. "It's amazing how the animals get to live, if only they realized how blessed they are to be in such an amazing environment." Carly says. "What do we know, maybe they do realize, maybe animals have more of a conscience than humans know." "I would not be surprised actually, maybe if humans got that all wrong." A cheerful look crossed both of their faces and the playful energy seems to be stronger than ever between the two of them.

The Elk family continued grazing, they even got pretty close to one of the younger ones, that happened to be closer to the trail. As they walk by though, it does not bother them, and it is beautiful to see just how innocent animals really are. They are just trying to live their lives peacefully and there is no need to fear even the mightiest of wildlife. You respect their living space, and they will respect you.

If the evergreen trees are big in the Seattle area, here they are like natural skyscrapers. They tower among them both, sending out a reminder of just how small we really are compared to the natural order of the universe. If they can grow to be so powerful without the help of man, it really is staggering how insignificant one human being really is compared to the full power of it all. They keep walking and a sense of eagerness begins to come upon both of them. Even though Bryce has done this trail several times, the picturesque setting never seems to get old. Everytime he comes out here it seems to shake up his view on life in a deeply shocking way. He comes back to his home feeling like he had just gone on a three-week vacation to some exotic mountain-filled country in Europe 10 hours away other than a less than three-hour car ride to some place in his own state. "I have a feeling we are getting pretty close to the final view" Carly joyfully exclaims. "From the look of it, on the mile track we are about three tenths of a mile away!"

The feeling of some gorgeous scenery about to appear on the trail is imminent. It is a mixture of feeling like three and a half miles have been walked as well as just a sense that comes from them both having done so many hikes. It also helps that it seems like they are out of such a dense forest, making it feel like an opening of something amazing is going to appear. It's like an epic sunset starting to form in the sky across the south Florida tropical shoreline.

A few minutes later, they came around a curve and there it was. A jaw-dropping array of the Cascade mountains right there in front of them. We look out together and both of us shine in glee. Almost like a mom seeing her newborn baby for the first time. For Carly, the excitement grows even stronger as this is her first time taking in the epic view. "What a world we have" Carly said, her voice more mellow for a moment than it was earlier in the day. "Bryce, you do not know how long I have waited, I am just speechless."

Then a moment later, Bryce walked closer to Carly. He looks into her eyes, just soaking in all the wonder she is filled with for a moment.

That second, Bryce feels a joy burst back in him, that joy feels as freeing as he did on the first day he really soaked in the nature of the Pacific Northwest with his friends as a kid. It is then he realizes that the beauty and joy he has inside him cannot be overtaken. He leans forwards towards her and reaches in for a huge kiss. They just stand there for a minute kissing as the mountains and open space illuminates the background. It showers their love for a moment in an all-consuming way that neither of them had ever experienced. It was from that kiss in which they fully embraced their time being. It was at that moment that it truly felt like whatever was going to happen to both of them in the future really did not matter. All that matters is, the beauty at this moment we have been given is meant to be fully embraced. The stars have us together right here for a reason, and that is one of the most amazing things life can offer us.

Carly checks her phone and notices it is already 3:15. The sun is still shining bright and for the past forty-five minutes all they did is sit there. The two of them found a fallen tree branch to relax on and they both just be still with each other, holding hands, with the birds chirping around, feeling like they are in their own little universe, all to themselves without a care in the world from the rest of any outside stressors. Bryce then wraps his arms around Carly, putting them into a sweet lingering cuddle. "This really has been one of the most amazing days in my life." Carly says, feeling so much comfort during the time they have at this park. "I just, I just have always wanted this, you know to be somewhere amazing like this, with a guy like you, who just gets me, I will never forget this moment Bryce, because you right now are giving me something my soul has longed for me. We are creating a memory that is going to be stored in both our hearts for as long as we walk on this planet." Bryce does not know what to say. A sense of utter beauty is among them right now and all he can do is hold her tightly. He then kisses her on the forehead and whispers, "Thank you for being the amazing woman you are." "Thank you for showing me just how special love can really be."

As they continue to sit on the giant tree branch, Carly rubs her pocket for a second. In her mind, she is randomly reminded that she has something to give Bryce. She then rushed back to a couple of days ago where she felt compelled to write something special. She remembers sitting on her dining room table, with her pajamas on, holding a pen and paper in her hand planning out a special statement. The spark came to her at around 10pm. She was finishing up her nightly routine and about to hop in bed when she felt led to put down some of her thoughts about all that had gone on recently. The emotion of writing it out flooded back into her. With her long blonde hair tied in a bun and the lights dimmed in her den, the moment becomes painfully vivid. She had to get her emotions out somewhere. Journaling has become something I love to do from time to time and I thought it was necessary to channel my feelings down whether he ends up seeing it or not. Writing words can convey so much power and I know that so well.

Growing up, Carly's favorite subject in highschool was actually English. Despite going on to major in computer programming, which also interested her. Technology has been a fascination of hers since she was little. Seeing how pop culture really has an influence on technology was really an interest too. In the end though, in all honesty, it seemed as though the computer world was calling her because of the better pay. While working in the writing world may have been a dream, this job and the salary allow me to do so many things for fun while off in my free time.

"I think we should start heading back soon. We have around a two-hour journey back," Bryce says. I could sense in his voice that he did not want to leave either. Bryce is a special man also, in the sense that he loves going out and doing fun things. I recently saw a Facebook post with these two guys from a podcast talking about how, generally speaking, straight guys do not like doing fun things. They went on to say we will go places with our women, like carnivals or apple picking at a farm in the Fall, to be nice, but they do not care to do those things. I think this is more of a stereotype, but you know what they say, there is some truth to stereotypes. Bryce really seemed to enjoy the activities though. That is another reason that if he moves, it will be very hard to deal with. He is such a rarity, in that instance, though a smile runs through myself, knowing I will probably, for many more years, I will have Britney and Sara to do those exciting things with.

They stood up from the trunk of the tree and stared around at the view one more time. Taking in every second of it all as we can. I then reach into my pocket, "I have something I need to give you." Carly says. "Please just don't open it until later, but there is something in there that is specifically for you." Bryce looks down at the large white envelope. It is a folded crease down the middle from it being shoved in her pocket the whole day. He gives it a shake, noticing it feels very light. He reads it and all that is written on the front is his name, beautifully written in cursive. He feels like there is some sort of document in there and that peaks his interest further. For a moment, he thinks maybe Carly thought about sharing some of her medical papers with him. I mean she did just have some pretty serious health issues. "Is everything ok with you?" Well that is a loaded question with everything happening between us lately, Carly thinks. She then replies, "Actually Bryce, Life has been messy recently, I cannot lie, but the truth is this letter should not give you anything to worry about and, yes, I am going to be just fine." They then smile at each other and begin the long hike back to where the day started.

The sun was starting to go down as they were on the trail which was bringing this one magical day to an end. They travel back through the deep woods and all the trees continue to cover them, creating a sense of utter bliss. It was like they had almost reached Nirvana, and they longed to keep the energy of today stored in their hearts, because somehow every moment of today was going to leave a deep impact on them by showing how, in the midst of brokenness, there is utter clarity to be found once you let go.

They make it back to the car just before full darkness begins to fill the land. The hint of sunshine still there fills the backdrop so that there still remains a tinge of light like a small candle burning bright in a dark room. Bryce begins to pull out and Carly lowers her hand down, resting it on his hand, holding it in a most gentle manner. "I will never forget this day, it was so perfect." Carly begins to realize just how sacred the time really was. It felt almost like a powerful date scene you found in a romance film. With love feeling perfect as a couple is in a beautiful setting just embracing each other, that is the feeling it brings. It is like romantic films offer a special type of movie, because what you feel bounces off the screen can be truly recaptured with another human. A connection like this is rare, but it is possible. Just though all movies make the way to the end credits, I sometimes realize real love plays out the same way. It is possible for it all to disappear.

The Seattle skyline begins to appear in the distance. All lit up, feeling like a complete contrast to the wilderness area they are making their way back from. It brightens the landscape, creating almost like a man made version of evergreen trees. While different, it creates its own unique beauty. As they get closer, they can feel the city energy about to come among them. They pass the skyscrapers that tower between them and realize how much they fail in comparison compared to the mountains minutes away. They are near Carly's apartment and a sense of bittersweet fills the car. It feels almost like the feeling of having to head to the airport after an exotic summer vacation somewhere in Europe. Sometimes the most special things in life can take place only a few hundred miles away though, and some of those you wish could last a lifetime.

"So I guess this is it then?" Carly asks, her voice becoming more mellow. Bryce does not say anything back, all he can do is look at her and stare. They glance deep into each other's eyes as an evening drizzle begins to fall, hitting the car in such a peaceful manner, creating a sense of tranquility. After a moment, the rain began to speed up, and it was clear it was about to get stormy. Finally, Bryce begins to speak, "Who knows, but even if it is, who is to say when something is an end? Maybe, despite whatever will happen, we will forever be together."

Carly wants to speak but she does not. Part of her wants to ask if he is moving out there, but really another part does not completely care to know. What would asking him for confirmation of this really even accomplish? The only thing it will do is add more pain. On the flip side, if he is staying it will add more joy, but is that really necessary? Today was such a beautiful moment in such a huge universe. And I truly believe our lives are already planned out. Like we all have a chosen path, so what difference will asking really make?

Carly then reaches her hand out and gently rubs Bryce's shoulder, before whispering in his ear, "Then if that's the case, I guess we can let it be a mystery for now." The thing is, life is this huge, insane, mystery. So many questions we are all faced with that we may never have the answers to. Why do some people come into our lives for a moment and others stay long term? Why do hard decisions get thrown at us at what sometimes seems like the worst instant possible? And why do we even come here if we are born to die? These big ideas and others ran through both of their minds as they sat in the car through some brief silence.

Carly then begins to step out of the car. A sense of coldness fills the area like a chill breeze falling in a remote forest at night. Although they are both trying to embrace the stunning day they shared, sometimes the anxiety of the future just won't let up. It takes a consuming toll on you like a tornado tearing through the open flat lands of Kansas. "Do not forget to read the letter Bryce, and I love you no matter what." Bryce's eyes begin to gently water, the emotions of everything that has gone on these past two weeks, up until now begin to come roaring into him like a huge wave coming onto the shores of Hawaii. "I love you too." She then walks towards the door and he loses it. With his hands on his steering wheel, all of his tears came streaming out, flowing like one of the mighty rivers in Olympic National Park.

He then feels a sense of anger and punches the steering wheel, "God he yells! Why is all this happening!" He feels helpless now, and realizes he is all alone again. Maybe some higher power is watching over him, but acknowledging that does that at all take away the emptiness. He then fiercely pulls off the parking spot and bolts his way onto the freeway to head back home. Before letting all his anger take over all of his being, memories flood of the time he and Carly have spent so far. From their first date at the park to the journey today, he takes a breath and tries to see all the beauty that has been sprinkled over his life and be apprecivice of it. It is like a movie is being played in his mind with the time they have been given and through it all once again, a sense of light begins to fill his spirit.

Chapter 28: Cathy

I felt a nudge in my heart to give my son a call. I have not heard from him in a while, and he usually gives me a call or text every couple of days. After our conversation recently when he came over for the weekend, I thought it would be great to check up on him. I give him a ring, but it goes to voicemail. I then decided to send a text message quickly, "Hey honey, please give me a call when you have a moment. Hope you have been doing OK xoxo." I then pressed send and set my phone down. I worry about Bryce probably more than I should, but knowing how sweet he is and everything he has faced, I think it is only natural. Also, it is great to have some great human connections. It gets lonely out here sometimes, and I do have a few friends that I truly adore, but Bryce and I share a special bond. Our hardships really added an unexpected beauty to our mother and son connection that not every parent has. I love talking to him too. We always have amazing conversations and that is always much better than scrolling on Facebook or Instagram. Nothing will ever replace the beauty of true human interaction. Call me old school, but talking on the phone is still such an amazing gift. All kids do these days is text and send stuff to each other on social media apps. Nothing wrong with that, but technology really has the power to disconnect us, especially with how invasive it is lately. Sometimes, I wish we could go back to a time without all these programs on our phone. To a time when we had to meet in person and could not just cherry-pick through photos of people on dating apps. Oh, and that do not even get me started. I truly believe they are meant to feed off of people's loneliness.

That does mean sometimes people do not get lucky and find someone they are really meant to be with, but at the core, those apps are there to make money. They want to keep you on them so they will have a strong user base and, in some ways, there is something more bad going on, and they are not all such beautiful businesses.

The other day, I stumbled upon a news article discussing how, right now, there is a huge revolution to stop using those apps. I am not at all surprised, and I am glad some people are waking up to the negative effects they can have on building connections. In a way, reading this started to give me hope for the world. With all the bad news you can see these days, that was a truly nice thing to see. There is a specialness to meeting someone the traditional way. To spot someone you are feeling drawn to and then trying to build a meaningful bond. It really is an amazing thing.

I will never forget the day Gerald reached out. We were both freshmen at Bellevue College, and we had the same English class together. It was 1982 and such a fun era. Seattle was truly booming and Eye Of The Tiger was playing everywhere. There were no smartphones, no food delivery apps like DoorDash, it really was a simpler time.

For a few classes I would notice him glancing over at me. I had a couple of amazing lady friends throughout college, and we were always giggling loudly as we exited the classroom. We were just a lively group. For some reason, out of the group of the four of us, Gerald was most drawn to me. One day, he just came up to me and basically said that I was beautiful and asked if I would be interested in going on a date with him to see ET on the big screen. I honestly felt flattered and so giddy. For one, I had not been on a date since I was 16. I was eager to have some alone time with a nice guy. I was by no means a desperate young lady, but when there is a guy that seems special, you better shoot your shot because a lot of times, he won't be single, for much longer.

Gerald really just seemed so sweet. For another, ET looked amazing. All the surrounding hype was incredible. You had to be there in the 80s just to understand how big of a thing movies actually were. There were no movies being treated as a fast cash grab or being sent straight to Netflix. No. Streaming was not even a thought yet. You went to the theater to experience an epic story on a huge silver screen.

After enjoying the movie with Gerald, I could not wait to get to know him more. When I think about that night seeing it at the theater, it brings back an epic sense of nostalgia. With the old-fashioned popcorn containers they had and the classic coke machines, what a fun time it was. The theater was completely sold out, which does not happen much for films these days. The movie really transported us to what seemed like a far off dimension. The sweet innocence of it mixed with the sci-fi elements really was so special. The magic ET brought was indescribable. The filmmakers definitely struck gold with creating it because I have not seen another movie like it over forty years later. I know I might sound old saying this, but I really do think they do not make movies like they did in the 80s anymore. I am not saying there are no good ones coming out sometimes now, but there was something special about that decade.

The beauty I felt being with Gerald was so stunning too. Being with him that night felt different from going to the theater with my group of girlfriends. He had such a mature vibe and I could tell already there was something different about him. Once the movie started, he whispered gently in my ear if he could hold my hand and I gently nodded with a bright smile. From that moment something bigger was telling me this man was a keeper. I loved that sweet gesture and when guys do little things like that, it means they actually see you more than just as something to us for a night of pleasure. When men just want sex from you, a lot of times there is a different energy you can sense. That night I was able to see that there are good guys out there. Us women are not the only ones that can have such a sweet nature and deep soul.

After the movie, he kissed me goodbye that night after dropping me off at home. I knew I could not wait to see him again. You know a first date is good when you have that feeling of not wanting it to end. I remember wishing we could go see another movie and just enjoy that whimsical feeling some more. Wishing that he could have come inside my house, and we just could have cuddled the whole night and be in each other's arms. I also know that it is beautiful to take the time to get to know each other so you can really build a life together that will be a life for both of us to really enjoy.

We ended up falling hard for one another after about two months of dating. By October that year it was like we were inseparable. We went on two different dates that fall to a farm with activities in Snohomish. I will never forget being among the open fields there full of pumpkins and feeling so young and free with Gerald. We ran through it with the cool air among us feeling so joyful. We then drank some warm apple cider from the food stand and cuddled next to each other on the bench, without a care in the world. It was such a beautiful time, both of those farm trips back in the 80s are things I will cherish in my heart forever.

Building that connection with him was such a special thing. You see Gerald actually coming up to me, and showing interest really was something that drew me to him. Back then, you had to do that. There was no other way. There was not any swiping across profiles or sending super likes that you had to pay for. It was a time when things had to happen more organically and honestly, what a beautiful thing that was.

I know relationships can still start this way in 2023, but it is just different. We are in a different era too, with so many people focused on the cynical stuff that is happening and full on feminism for women. I mean look, we even had a female vice president. It really is a different world now, but we can never forget the beauty of human love. How special it is to have someone that fully gets you and embraces you for who you are. Someone to go to fun places with and share every holiday of each season. Someone who will cuddle you at night and be there for you when you are sick. Because they can be gone in an instant, and if anyone knows that well enough it would be me.

I headed upstairs to my bedroom. After hopping into my bed, I opened my nightstand drawer. I keep a couple of books I am reading there and a few other things like my iPad. I also store some artwork that Steven and Bryce made for me when they were in elementary school. There is one that Bryce painted for me of a beach and sunset. He made it shortly after the Caribbean adventure we went on. Seeing that image always makes me feel so happy. I also keep some special notes there that I have saved from Gerald. The night after he had proposed, he had given me a handwritten letter. I always love to revisit it from time to time just to feel some love. I pulled it out and started reading,

Dear Cathy,

How did I get so lucky? From the moment I had laid eyes upon you in college five years ago, I thought you were the most beautiful lady ever. Yes, you looked gorgeous, but I also could not help but admire your bubbly confidence. I could tell you had fun and were exactly the person you are whether people liked it or not. People loved you and I could see how much you added to that friend group just by being true to yourself. Thank you for saying yes to my proposal because, in all honesty, you did not have to. I am so happy you did though. Each day I have fallen more and more in love with you. I promise to always keep you safe. To make sure that beautiful smile of yours never fades away. To be the best husband ever and build an amazing future with you. I cannot wait to experience the awesome life we will have together. You are the most confident, caring and strong person I have ever met, and you are going to be the best mama ever. Keep shining my love, I promise to never let go of you for as long as I am breathing on this earth. Wedding day is coming summer 1995!!!! Cannot wait! Hope you are excited too, my love!

Love you so much, Gerald

I begin to tear up. Everytime I read through it I feel like a part of him will live on forever through those words. I am so grateful for that. A little bit later, I got a text back from Bryce,

"Hey mom, I will call you back tomorrow, a lot going on lately."

My heart then aches for him because he is struggling now and all I want to do is be there for my sweet son. He and Steven are all I have left and a part of Gerald is still there through them. I know he will always need his mom to an extent. Family is the touchstone to a beautiful life. I then typed out my reply,

"Ok sweetie, I am here for you, please call me ASAP love, mom."

Chapter 29: Gerald

February 2003, 1 month before my passing

Cancer is a strange thing some of us humans unfortunately have to experience. I think one of the craziest things about it is that doctors can actually tell, almost to the day, when it will be time for your last breath. Yes, sometimes they are wrong, but you have to remind yourself that there is a chance you won't beat it. It is like they have the crystal ball into when you will pass on from here. In many ways, it is both terrifying and comforting. It is comforting in the sense that I can do my best to embrace the time I will have left with Cathy, Steven and Bryce. I want to stay positive though, I believe the power of God has the final say. Who knows though, maybe us believers in a higher power are wrong about everything and there is no strong being who controls it all. I have always had faith. I think it is important to know there is something bigger in this life than just us humans, but as I am nearing the end of my life, almost every day, I cannot help to think if God is just something we created to give ourselves some comfort.

Cathy, I know will be okay. While she is super loving and compassionate, she is also the strongest woman I have ever known. That is what I loved about her. You can tell she had a big heart to share, but she also has an underlying strength that is just so beautiful. When we first met years ago, I can just tell she had a unique soul. Even when she was 19 when we met, there was just something different about her. She had maturity that was more like someone in their early 30s. Strength and sweetness do not always go hand in hand. She really was a full-rounded human that did not just try to identify as one thing. Even back in the 80s, you had tougher ladies and more sweet and sensitive ones. People may evolve a little but generally speaking, they do not change all that much. Seeing Cathy so boldly embrace her caring side while being a happy and confident, independent woman drew me towards really wanting to build a life together and also added a special sexiness too.

Steven I feel is going to be just fine as well. I guess he inherited more of his mother's strength because he seems to have more of that. He is able to let things go more. About a month ago, he was dealing with a bully. Steven is a first-year student now in high school and let me just tell you, from middle school to the early years of high school, kids can be so cruel. This one kid wrote a demeaning word on his locker with a black sharpie. Some people would have been upset, but Steven just brushed it off. Came home and told us about it and how ignorant some people are and said bullies are just insecure people, and he would never take them personally. Now, even though he can brush things off more and stand strong on his own, that does not mean he still does not have a heart. He loves to make people laugh and is sweet but in a more confident way. I know he is still going to have to grieve the loss of me too. Losing a parent before graduating from high school is not something a lot of kids go through. I could not even imagine going through that. It is going to be hard on everyone to a certain extent.

Bryce, though, is the one I worry about the most. Even at just seven years old, it is amazing that I can already see his true personality. He is very soft and sweet, and I can tell he is different from most guys already. It is funny. Sometimes I think about what career path he will choose once he graduates from high school and one that keeps coming to my mind is being a therapist. I can see him going day in and day out, fiercely wanting to help people overcome their issues. Even one time already, when his good friend, Chase, lost his pet lizard, Bryce showed such a powerful compassion for him during the time of loss. He would comfort his friend and even invite him over a couple nights after the passing for a video game hangout. Chase did not have a PlayStation 2 yet, and he thought that would cheer his buddy up during his difficult time.

I am not saying that will be what he chooses, but I can see him being an excellent one. He has an empathy that I can already see is really special. I hope he will be okay when I leave. That sweet nature he possesses is why I worry so much. I have been trying to embrace every moment I have left with him though. To show him that his old man will always love him and be there for him in spirit.

Even though a lot of times I feel weak, I try to make each moment enjoyable for the three of us. The other day we had a movie night. I told Cathy to pick up all the junk food snacks she could from the grocery store and I let Bryce pick whatever movie he wanted to from video on demand. Cathy came in with bags of pretzels, cheese doodles and others, as well as over 10 boxes of candy. I remember Bryce looking so happy when all the delicious treats were poured out on the table. He then ended up choosing Ice Age and we had a blast watching. Munching away on so many cookies and potato chips and seeing my little man smile when Sid the sloth did something silly was the most beautiful thing. I can not believe how gorgeous the animation looked too. All the 3D styling these movies now have is truly incredible. What an upgrade from just less than 10 years ago when a lot of them still used that 2D style. I remember when I was a kid the shows looked so crappy compared to how beautiful of a job the animators do now. Comparing The Flintstones to something like Toy Story 2 is like comparing apples to oranges. They look stunning now. Speaking of Toy Story, which is my son's favorite film. The Buzz Lightyear toy is his absolute favorite. We have a blast playing with it together over in our toy room. Seeing him smile as the toy goes "And to infinity and beyond" makes me smile more than I ever had before. I think not being able to do that with him will be one of the biggest things I miss once my time on earth runs out.

I tucked my little man in that night and read him a short bedtime book. I was feeling so fatigued from the disease eating away at my body, but again, I just have to push through it because I do not know how many more days I will be blessed with. As I finished pulling up the blanket onto him, he began to slowly speak "Daddy, I don't want you to leave me, Steven and mommy, I don't know what I will do without you." His voice had a tinge of depression in it. At that moment, I couldn't help but to start crying. I wipe them and think I can't believe this. Why is life doing this to us? Not even me, but my little boy. Why does he have to go through this? It is not fair. There is nothing like having a family. It makes you see how precious life really is and how being there for other humans is so important. Once you have kids, you begin to see so many of the things you thought were important, like partying, working, buying material things, really do not matter at all. Seeing my little man grow and enjoy having fun was the most amazing thing to witness.

"I know, I do not want to leave you either, but some things in life we have absolutely no say over, and I am here with you right now. You are going to do so many amazing things in this world, Bryce. You can do anything you want."

He then just looks at me and then gives me a hug. He started to cry too. We then just sat there on his little bed. At that moment, I do not care that I am not feeling too well. I decide to just be there cuddling with him until he ends up falling asleep.

It was about thirty minutes until I could tell he was off in his sweet little dreams and I had to rest there for a few more minutes before I could muster up the strength to get up. I then looked around the room and marveled at all the sweet innocence that comes with being young. Even the room has a special quality in it that most adult bedrooms lack. With his outer space wallpaper surrounding us, it brings a calmness to my racing mind. I then realize from his room how big the universe is, how it goes on forever. It then reminds me of how I believe that is all how we are too. That there is so much more going on than just our physical bodies here. I then whispered to Bryce through my tears,

"You do not have to worry buddy, we are all infinite." I do not think he heard me, but maybe he did. Just saying that gently out loud though, it needed to be done right now.

Chapter 30: Bryce

I had finally made it home. After such an adventurous day, I felt completely wiped out. The feeling of being home felt as nice as a relaxing day chilling on the gorgeous shore of Waikiki Beach, Hawaii. As I walked in, and opened his door, an envelope fell out of my pocket. I looked down and remembered it was the one Carly had given me. For a second, I had almost forgotten about it. I quickly picked it up and walked over to my dining room table and set it down. Part of me wanted to open it now, but the tiredness of such an adventurous hiking trip and long day of driving was all consuming. I then walked over to my bedroom and plopped down on the bed. Before even taking my clothes off or brushing my teeth, in what seemed like almost an instant second, I had fallen asleep.

I woke to the sun shining through my windows. The light fills my room with a sense of lovely brightness that comes along at the start of each day. Every sunrise is a reminder of hope. A sign that there is going to be goodness in life and that light also signals the start of new possibilities. I must have been truly exhausted because, even on weekends, I am up before the sun starts peeking through. What is beautiful, though, I realized, is that this was a different type of exhaustion. Not one from a hectic day at the office, but one from an unforgettable day with a truly amazing person.

I got out of bed, and started the Keurig machine to have a nice cup of coffee. I like to have some coffee, mainly on the weekends, to really take a moment to slow down and soak in the peacefulness that comes with a couple of days off. Ever since I moved out from college, it has become somewhat of a habit. The machine stops brewing and I reach over to my refrigerator for some creamer. I then grab some sugar from the cabinet. Nice and light like a sweet summer day is the only way I will enjoy my weekend drink.

I headed over to the kitchen table and took a slow sip of it. The warmth of the coffee fills me with invigorating feelings, almost like catching powerful sun rays down on Zuma beach in Malibu on a sunny summer day. I then glance over and happen to see the letter from Carly sitting right there. With my name written in bold black letters, and it sealed completely, I felt so compelled to open it. Another thing that added to my intrigue was the fact that it was a handwritten letter from 2023. Who even does that anymore? Like emails are barely a thing, getting a long text message is rare these days. The romantic in me thought this was all too sweet. I can never deny my love for warm mushy stuff. This was one of the most sappy and cute things someone could do for me.

I took a breath and then finally began to pull open the letter. The envelope was sealed pretty tight to my surprise, without waiting anymore, I unfolded and began to read.

Dear Bryce,

I would first like to apologize if this comes off as a little weird but knowing the man you are I thought you might appreciate a handwritten letter, even in an era where nobody does them much. Second, I just want to say thank you. Thank you for the time you have chosen to spend with me. I also would like to point out right off the bat, I still am uncertain what the future holds for the two of us, and that is completely fine. I have come to accept the fact that these past several weeks have been filled with such wonderful beauty and I am forever grateful I have gotten to experience this with you. As soon as I saw your profile on Bumble, I could tell you were different. There were no pictures with you trying to impress me with a six pack of abs, or out at some lavish nightclub partying like crazy with your buddies. None of that. What I noticed was a cute Pacific Northwest guy that radiated magical energy. One that loved nature and just appeared to be so sweet. One that in an era where technology makes it so easy to swipe and find a quick night of fun, you wanted a woman to call your own. Someone to cherish and to have by your side. Once we had our first date at Discovery Park, I had a feeling I was right. As I got to know you more, my previous assumptions were true. You are a sweet man with a heart of gold. You helped me to see that love is a special part of life. And while going out and living life to the fullest is a very important part of it all, so is having someone to cherish. That having someone who sees your worth really does make a difference for it all. Though our connection may have been short lived and filled with a fair amount of pain, I assure you that it still meant the world. I feel like it was one of the most life changing experiences I have had thus far. Not everyone finds someone that from the first meeting, it seems like they so naturally get you. You saw my beauty in a way beyond most guys'. You did not just see me for my looks, or find my personality off putting. I appreciate the person you are. Even at times when you showed the deep emotional side you possess, I was able to see you hold so much greatness. You have also shown me that I have a depth in me that I did not even realize was there. I now know that when someone chooses you as their own, it adds something special to both of the individuals lives. I hope you are happy and successful in whatever path you choose because at the end of the day we all have our own destinies to follow. Just know if you choose to stay here in the evergreen state, we can build a life together. Love you forever my sweet man.

With love, Carly

I then feel my eyes begin to water up. Before I know it, a tear falls and drops right onto the letter. A few more begin to fall and end up filling the letter with a dampness. I notice they are not just tears of sadness though, a lot of them are tears of joy. The joy of realizing how amazing she is and that she accepts me no matter what. Tears of looking back over the time we have gotten together and realizing how special it was.

I look back up at the part where it was written how we have some pain together, but I then see that all the pain would not have happened if it had not been for how powerful love really was. From the first date, to the amazing taco night, every fun moment we shared had a sense of purity. A sense that we both could be exactly who we are, and the other did not care. That for me, especially, I could be the sensitive and emotional man I am, and I would not be shamed. That is special. And from whatever happens here on out, I can be happy to know that I learned that I can be fully who I am and still be loved. Because isn't that what love is? Someone seeing you in your most authentic form and still embracing your true soul.

It is around 1:30 now and the sun is still shining as bright as ever. I checked the weather app on my phone and saw it is going to be a stunning eighty degrees today and I feel like it is too beautiful to spend the day cooped up here. We are in Washington right now, the hub for outdoor activities. I then decided it would be nice to do some hiking at Discovery Park. There really are tons of trails there and much more to discover. Another thing Carly has re-added to my life was a sense of appreciation for where I live. From being so busy with life pretty much since high school, I had really forgotten to slow down sometimes. It was not even just that park I noticed too, but all of Seattle. For a late afternoon adventure, it being so close with much to see, also felt like the perfect idea. A solo hike can give me some more confidence too, after all which has gone down.

I headed over to the park and made it back to the lighthouse. Some clouds have come out into the sky, adding a bit less sunshine, filling the area with the perfect mix of added Pacific northwest moody energy. I then decided to walk right and head towards the other stretch of beach I had not yet uncovered. I walked past the lighthouse and rocks and a sense of inner strength began to fill me. A liberation I never knew I had started to come through. I guess being alone in nature after going through such a wild ride with Carly is really helpful now.

I walked a little bit further down before heading up into a forest trail. The lush greenery surrounds the area, and it is hard to believe a major city is just minutes away. Right now, it just feels like me and the wilderness with the peace that comes from it all. As I continued walking deeper in the forest, I began to hear a group of people giggling. It sounds like so much joy they are filled with. I think it is a group of girls. You know that song Girls Just Wanna Have Fun? Well I feel like there is some truth to that. For some reason, a lot of women seem to have a lot more fun moments than guys. That is always nice to see.

Adding some silliness and joy to life is so important. If I have learned anything lately, it is that when you love deeply, you can go through a lot of hard pain, but it is important to keep your happiness a big priority. As the group appears closer, I begin to notice something. I cannot believe what I saw. Oh, I definitely know one of those girls. How in the name of the universe is Carly again?

<u>Chapter 31: Carly</u>

I meet his eyes and cannot believe it is him again. It all feels so surreal, almost like I am stuck in this dream that won't let go. After writing the letter, part of me almost thought of it as a final goodbye. That everything that is going to happen is out of my hands and that I should just focus on what is in front of me. Once again, though, fate is taking my life by storm. "You guys cannot get away from each other, this is too cute," Sara says. I don't even know what to say to anyone. I stood there in utter shock. I glanced over at Britney and Sara before staring directly into his eyes. The deep woods are surrounding us and that adds a mystical, almost fairy tale-like energy as this wild situation unfolds. Here I am having a fun day going to the arcade and then hiking and bang, it is like God is showing me how small I really am. All the fun escapism of today is gone, and now real life is back at us. The power of love and how there is so much more to life than just living it up is standing face to face with us.

"Uh, can you guys go do another hike? Or maybe go hang out at a bar or someplace I am so sorry if I sound rude, this is just crazy. You know this is not like me to push you guys away like this. I will meet you back in the car later." "We got it Carly, just do not get back there too late.' Britney says "I won't, do not worry, I will see you guys soon."

"So we meet again, Ms. O'connor." Bryce says in a subtly playful manner. "Yup once again, in the most random of places, in the middle of the woods at a giant park." "Maybe not too random, as we did have our first date here." "Well then that makes it just all the weirder." "It is like I cannot get away from you. Which is not a bad thing, I just do not know where everything stands for the two of us."

We then began to walk towards the water outside of the woods. A sense of speechlessness covers both of us. It is like something bigger wanted us to see each other again. Maybe just for another moment, or maybe for longer, who knows anything anymore. I have learned lately that I cannot control a lot of aspects in life and trying to hold on to control so much is the quickest way to rid a lot of the amazing parts of this journey we are on. Sometimes you have to let things work out in the way they are meant too. All I know is right here, in this beautiful park, a man I truly admire is placed here for us to spend some more time together.

The sense of quietness continues among us. It is a special feeling going on right now that almost feels like a bit of magic. It is like we cannot say much, and all we can do is be in each other's presence. I have never felt anything like it in my life. The moment feels like a scene in a romance movie. Where it is just the two main characters in a loving state. When there is not much dialogue happening, you can just sense the love of them pouring out of the screen. Right now, our love feels like hot glue, meshing the two of us together, reminding us in a powerful way how rare this type of bond really is. Bryce then grabs my hand and pulls out of the forest as we arrive at the beach. The lush trees disappear and the beautiful shoreline is located in front of our view. I notice him glance around for a moment, kind of looking like he is trying to find something, and then he just begins to kiss me. They kiss for about a minute before lying down on the sand. This time there was no blanket for the two of them, just the rustic sand mixed with the trees behind us in the background.

We lay there beside each other with their hands clasped together. Just being there by the water as the evening sun shines. The warmth of the sun has more of a gentle feeling as the temperature has started to drop. Once again, the romantic energy between us is utterly powerful, but this time it feels even different. It is like a magnetic force wanting us to be close. To embrace this connection with no boundaries. Right now, nothing else matters. Not the job offer that has been pounding him. Not Britney or Sara. Not the projects that have to be done at work. All that matters is this beauty right now.

I then roll over and Bryce wraps me in a gentle cuddle right there. At the moment, I think we both probably look like two teenagers experiencing their first love together, but I know this is both our first magical connection, and that can occur at any age. I did not know true love would actually feel this amazing. There is something so perfect about the way it feels in his arms. It really does feel like we are two characters in a romance novel with a fantasy-like love. Also, who cares what people may think, not everyone can understand your full feelings and people have their own crap to worry about anyway. Right now, our little love is for us and the freedom we feel now feels like my inner child coming out in a way I have never felt in some time.

We just lay there and a sense of coziness continues to overflow every moment. "I cannot believe you are here again." He whispers in my ear. "I am so happy that we are back together, we are free now, do not worry about anything." We stay there and bask in the sunlight, even as it begins to get dimmer. The light is there among us, adding an extra special feel as it casts a light on the water in front of us. I know how important it is to embrace every second now. If you do not, you might miss the awesome thing that is right in front of your face.

I try not to focus on the darkness caving in from the sky, but it is hard because I do not want us to get lost on our way back. There are not many streetlights. It does get pretty desolate out here. I then rolled over on top of him and looked into his piercing blue eyes. "Want to go back to my place for the night?" I asked him. I then lower myself and give him a quick kiss on his freshly shaved cheek. It is going to be getting fully dark soon, and it might be nice to lie in an actual bed together after being here on the sand for almost two hours. Maybe we can take a shower with each other too to get all the dirt off. I then hear my phone ding and pull it out. I see it is a text from Britney which reads

"Had to head out to get some dinner, we tried waiting, but it was getting late, hope you are having a nice time."

Shoot. They left. "Uh, Bryce. I just found out the girls had left. Would you be able to give me a ride home?" A silence fell between us for a moment. For some reason, he does not say anything right away, but that is ok. Whatever happens, happens. I know I will find a way home. Life always makes a way for us. Even if I had to take an Uber, it would be fine. After a little bit of silence, he then squeezes me a bit tighter. Eventually, He whispers in my ear, "All we have is now. Please just be here with me." I kiss him not gently on his lips before falling by his side as he wraps me in his strong arms. Oh, how right he is. We do just have this moment and what a horrible thing it would be to try and rush it away, because you never know when something so amazing will come to an end. Today could be all you get, and from now on I am going to start fully taking in every single second that I am breathing.

Acknowledgements

First off, I have to thank God! I truly believe it is you and only you who has brought me to a place where I actually had a concept for a novel and then was able to bring it to fruition! Thank you for all the beauty you have put into my life over these past five years. I am in awe every day of what you are doing to my life for your glory and everything I have overcome. Thank you from the bottom of my heart. Writing a book takes a lot of dedication and everything He has brought me through has led me to this point in my life and writing career. My sister Angela. Thanks for listening to all my thoughts and ideas about this project on our late night calls. Including my crazy dream of having Sydney Sweeney and Timothee Chalamet play Carly and Bryce lol Love you buddle :) Anyone who has ever said I am a good writer or has read any of my other previous works, whether on my personal blog or the magazine I freelance write for Out In Jersey, thank you so much! Your support means everything and I do this for the people! Whether it is with More To Life, with wanting to tell a moving romance story, or with the entertainment journalism work I do, this is all for the readers! I hope you loved my first book and had a wonderful experience reading it! Speaking of Out In Jersey, I have to thank you all so much too! Special shoutout to the boss people, Peter and Maria! You guys are incredible to work with and have taught me so much about professional writing! It is an honor to work alongside you all in creating an awesome publication. I am so grateful to play a small part in helping the magazine come to life for all of our readers. All of my amazing friends, Fran. Thank you for our special friendship. I am so grateful we met in that Film Buffs group on Facebook. I never thought I would ever find a friend that has such a similar movie and book taste. As well as one who just in general feels such a special connection. Love you so much and forever grateful our souls cross paths! Lauren, Serena, Katie, Allison, Evan, among others! You are some of the best people ever and really are my chosen family. So happy we have each other to make our lives a little better and more fun! Love getting to share stories with you at our quarterly movie nights too. It is so cool to have many of you who appreciate art as much as I do. Whether that be books, films or metal music (I'm looking at you for the last one bestie Lauren,) ;) Thank you to the romance fans! As one myself, I really hope I did not let you down with this book! I really tried to capture and create elements in a story that I thought you guys would love. Lol. You are all some of the best fans in the world! I know I may be biased BUT it is true! <3 Love you guys. Thank you to my writing influences who partially inspired me to write my own book. The king Nicholas Sparks. How do you do it?! I don't know, but you sure have a gift and if I even came close to writing as good a romance as you can, I could die happy. I will never forget seeing your book to film adaptation, Dear John, on the big screen when I was 12 and ever since then I have been hooked on all your work. John Green. The Fault In Our Stars is one of my favorite books and movies ever. You really shifted the landscape of romance stories once the film came out. You impacted the film industry and a whole few years of teen romances followed and you have influenced me and many other authors with the way we tell stories. It is one that really left a life-changing mark on me and so many others, and really played a role in partially shaping the type of stories I yearn to tell. Thank you for creating that powerful masterpiece that is way more than just a teen romance. Gayle Forman. Oh, and I recently discovered you started as an entertainment journalist too, and that is incredible. You are such an inspiring human and gifted storyteller. Thank you for your incredible and poignant work. My nephews Luke and Connor! You all bring soooo much joy to my life. I love you both to pieces and love getting to be your uncle. My cousin Russell and his wife Dominique. We may not talk too much but whenever I see you both it's always a joy. Thanks for your kind words over too these past couple of years. I always appreciate you guys exactly how you are. Thank you to Amazon Self publishing services . OK, but seriously, despite all the negative things people say about your company, this is such a beautiful thing you do. Giving writers such easy accessibility to releasing a book that we used to not have. This is amazing, so thank you for the service you guys offer. My dad and his fiancé, Dani. Appreciate all of your words of encouragement as well throughout this journey. Lastly, thank you to anyone who finished reading this novel. If you did, please know I am eternally grateful. I do not know how many people this story will reach, but when I started writing, I truly thought even if one person reads it and has a life-changing impact, that would be enough. I would be amazed to know that someone experienced a story that I felt so compelled to write. That is not to say I would not want it to grow to more readers, but at the end of the day, some things are out of our control, and I am just in awe that I actually finished a book and someone like you took the time to actually care about these words and immerse themselves into Carly and Bryce's romantic journey! Hope you enjoyed your time with them in the beautiful Pacific Northwest region of America! Love to you all, Nicholas xoxo

About the Author

Nicholas Attanasio has loved stories for his whole life. Whether it be music from when he was a young kid, or when he became a true dedicated lover of film and books when he was 12, it was always a dream of his to also be a part of creating his own art for people to enjoy. More To Life is his debut adult romance novel. His work can also be found in Out In Jersey magazine where is a freelance entertainment journalist with them. He also has his own movie review blog on wordpress which can be found at https://nicksentertainmentreviews.wordpress.com/   Now, with being a published romance author, Nicholas longs to tell stories that will leave a lasting inspiring impact on the reader's heart. When he is not working on writing pieces, he also runs a pet sitting business watching people's dogs and cats. In his free time Nicholas is an almost too overly obsessed fan of watching movies and reading books, where romance is one of his favorite genres in both of those formats. He loves experiencing movies on the big screen and tries to see as many as possible in the theater. Concerts are another one of his favorites activities to attend. You can also find him traveling fun places, especially one of his favorites, the Western side of America or experiencing the nature of the northeast, closer to where he lives in New Jersey, during his time off.